Chatting With Girls Like You

Books by
Sandra Byrd
FROM BETHANY HOUSE PUBLISHERS

Girl Talk
Chatting With Girls Like You
A Growing-Up Guide
The Inside-Out Beauty Book
Stuff 2 Do

The Hidden Diary
Cross My Heart
Make a Wish
Just Between Friends
Take a Bow
Pass It On
Change of Heart
Take a Chance
One Plus One

Sandra Byrd

chatting
WITH GIRLS
Like
YOU

61 MORE
Real-Life Questions
With Answers
FROM THE BIBLE

Chatting With Girls Like You
Copyright © 2004
Sandra Byrd

Cover design by Melinda Schumacher

Unless otherwise identified, Scripture quotations are from the *International Children's Bible, New Century Version,* copyright © 1986, 1988 by Word Publishing, Dallas, Texas 75039. Used by permission.

Scripture quotations identified NIV are from the HOLY BIBLE, NEW INTERNATIONAL VERSION®. Copyright © 1973, 1978, 1984 by International Bible Society. Used by permission of Zondervan Publishing House. All rights reserved.

Scripture quotations identified NLT are from the *Holy Bible,* New Living Translation, copyright © 1996. Used by permission of Tyndale House Publishers, Inc., Wheaton, Illinois 60189. All rights reserved.

Scripture quotations identified TLB are from *The Living Bible* © 1971 owned by assignment by Illinois Regional Bank N.A. (as trustee). Used by permission of Tyndale House Publishers, Inc., Wheaton, IL 60189. All rights reserved.

All rights reserved. No part of this publication may be reproduced, stored in a retrieval system, or transmitted in any form or by any means—electronic, mechanical, photocopying, recording, or otherwise—without the prior written permission of the publisher and copyright owners.

Published by Bethany House Publishers
11400 Hampshire Avenue South
Bloomington, Minnesota 55438
www.bethanyhouse.com

Bethany House Publishers is a Division of
Baker Book House Company, Grand Rapids, Michigan.

Printed in the United States of America

Library of Congress Cataloging-in-Publication Data

Byrd, Sandra.
   Chatting with girls like you : 61 more real-life questions with answers from the Bible / by Sandra Byrd.
     p. cm.
   ISBN 0-7642-2754-8 (pbk.)
   1. Girls—Religious life—Miscellanea—Juvenile literature. 2. Christian life—Biblical teaching—Miscellanea—Juvenile literature. I. Title.
   BV4551.3.B95   2004
   248.8'2—dc22
                                                                         2004005571

SANDRA BYRD lives near beautiful Seattle, between snow-capped Mount Rainier and the Space Needle, with her husband and two children (and let's not forget her golden retriever, Duchess). When she's not writing, she's usually reading, but she also likes to scrapbook, listen to music, and spend time with friends. Besides writing *Chatting With Girls Like You,* she's also the author of THE HIDDEN DIARY books and the bestselling series SECRET SISTERS.

Contents

Part One: Friends   11

Part Two: Myself   33

Part Three: Faith   55

Part Four: Family   77

Part Five: Society   99

Part Six: School   121

*All Scripture is inspired by God
and is useful to teach us what is true
and to make us realize what is wrong in our lives.
It straightens us out and teaches us to do what is right.
It is God's way of preparing us in every way,
fully equipped for every good thing God wants us to do.*

2 Timothy 3:16–17 NLT

Let's chat!
I'm glad you're here!

What is Chatting With Girls Like You, *anyway?*

It's a book of questions from everyday life with answers that you can put to work right away. Girls are curious and intelligent and want to solve the problems they face each day. Girls—not adults—wrote each and every question.

Are these the only answers from the Bible?

No. The Bible is chock-full of good things to say—more than a thousand pages of it! But the Bible doesn't ever disagree with itself. These are some good answers from the Bible. You'll have to keep studying it over a lifetime so you know more and more of what God has to say. He wants to talk to you every day. Every time you read the Bible you will learn something new. Every day you will encounter new situations, new circumstances. If you know to go to the Bible, you will always have God's answer. Keep reading and listening till you understand. God talks to us in the Bible. His Word is alive.

If you have more questions after reading this book, you might want to get ahold of my book *Girl Talk*. It covers a different set of questions, all important to girls.

How do I get started?
Turn the page!

Part One

Friends

As iron sharpens iron, a friend sharpens a friend.
Proverbs 27:17 NLT

Girls Like You Wonder...

1. Why do my friends fight over who gets to be the leader—even if it's just a feeling and not said with words?

2. Why are some girls mean sometimes and nice sometimes?

3. Do I have to share my things (and my family!) even when I don't want to?

4. How do you know if someone is a true friend?

5. What can I do if someone wears weird clothes and stuff but keeps trying to be friends with me?

6. Is there anything I can do if the populars whisper secrets about me?

7. How do you know whom to invite to a party, whom to leave out, and how to do it all nicely?

8. What can I do if one friend wants to hog me all the time?

9. Is it okay if friends are angry with one another?

10. Can I help make my friend a better Christian? Can someone make me a better Christian?

Friends

The girls in my class are my friends, but we often fight over silly stuff like who gets to be the leader of our plans. Why can't we just take turns?

Preschoolers have to learn how to take turns. They're grabby—they take what they want no matter who else wants it. They cut in line and don't care who sees. They play with a toy for a long time, even if someone is waiting. Usually, a parent or a teacher steps in to make them share.

When kids are older, like you are, being selfish isn't so obvious. It's being left out because you didn't play by the leaders' unspoken rules. Someone takes the best prize at a party. People pout and punish if their ideas aren't followed. As you get older, the adults around you tend to see less, because selfishness is happening under the surface. You're not supervised as much. That can actually be a good thing. Why? Because it allows *you* to be a leader by making Christlike choices rather than being forced to by an adult.

Christianity is the upside-down faith. The world says, "Get as much as you can." Jesus says, "Give away your coat." The world says, "Keep away from unpopulars." Jesus says, "Visit the sick and those in prison." The world says, "Get your turn." Jesus says, "Those who are first will be last." Choose friends who aren't going to be bossy all of the time. Those kinds of people don't easily change. But within a group of friends, start leading upside down. Let others choose the game. Sit quietly until you're asked what you'd like. Go to the back; take the smallest prize. You'll be surprised. When you stop looking out for yourself and are interested in others, many people will rally around to be interested in *you!* Think of it like a snow globe. When it's right-side up, it looks okay. When you turn it upside down, you can see beautiful things you didn't see before.

Chatting With Girls Like You

List three ways you can be an upside-down leader in your family or group of friends.

1.

2.

3.

Everyone who makes himself great will be made humble. But the person who makes himself humble will be made great.
LUKE 14:11

Friends

Why do some girls like you one day and then the next day they're mean to you? I don't know what to do about it.

Well, the first thing you have to do is define what "mean" is. When I have a problem, I first look at myself and my own behavior. Give it a try. Were you coming on too strong? Did a girl invite you to do one thing and then you wanted to do everything with her? If so, she might have chilled things down a bit to get some space. It wouldn't feel good, but it wouldn't be mean.

However, if you've checked yourself out and found that your behavior is okay, then look at the other girl. What happens when a gardener plants a lemon tree? It grows up and soon produces lemons. First, only one or two lemons appear. They might even look like limes or oranges at first, from a distance, or it looks like just a plain old tree. As the tree gets more and more established, more lemons grow. Soon the tree is covered with lemons. It's clearly a lemon tree.

When you first get to know someone, you assume the best. She's probably nice. She wants to be kind. You do a few things with her. Maybe one or two lemons pop out, but overall, good things are happening. However, as you spend more and more time with her and watch her in action, you see more lemons. Even if she tries to fake being nice, it won't work very long. Why not? Because she's growing lemons in her heart, not just in her actions.

Jesus said that whatever is in the heart of a person comes out through his or her mouth. A lemon tree can't fake being an orange tree by painting its fruit orange. Soon enough you'd take a bite and know it was a lemon. In the same way, a truly mean-hearted person can fake good words or deeds when it benefits her, but she can't cover it up forever. What's in her heart will always come out.

Don't waste your time trying to change this person from a lemon tree to an orange tree. Only God can do that. Don't waste your time wondering *why* this person is a lemon tree. She is. Instead, look around you and find a nice apple, pear, peach, or

Chatting With Girls Like You

cherry tree to befriend. Until she allows God to change her heart, a mean person is always going to serve lemons.

Is there a friend you keep trying to please so she'll be kind to you?

Are you able to change a lemon tree into an orange tree? Can you change another person's heart by anything you do?

> *A tree is identified by its fruit. Make a tree good, and its fruit will be good. Make a tree bad, and its fruit will be bad. . . . For whatever is in your heart determines what you say. A good person produces good words from a good heart, and an evil person produces evil words from an evil heart.*
> MATTHEW 12:33–35 NLT

Friends

My family has an exchange student living with us this summer. From now on, it will be for six weeks every summer! I don't want to share my room with her. I really don't want to be her friend. What can I do?

It's not easy to take the normal rhythm of your house and suddenly change tunes. Your family becomes like a little band—everyone knows what instrument he or she plays and plays his or her part. Your family gets used to having a drum, a guitar, a piano, and a flute. It's beautiful music and a comfortable sound.

Now a clarinet has moved in. Things feel and sound kind of strange. Not what you're used to. You always did fine without a clarinet, and now you have to make room in your music for *her* parts. She squeaks and squawks sometimes. You have to find pieces that include parts for a clarinet. Everybody has to shuffle around her.

That's kind of what it feels like when a foreign exchange student moves into your home. Suddenly your parents have to make time for her. You change your family schedule to accommodate her needs, too. She sounds funny. She doesn't like your food, which makes her seem like an ingrate. She not only has to share your room, but she wants to *change* your room! I don't blame you for not wanting to be her friend.

But if you look at it from her point of view, it's really scary. She's changed her whole band. She can feel your vibe—you don't like her so much. It makes her feel vulnerable. The food is weird. She can't understand what people are saying. She doesn't know when to talk and when to be quiet or what to wear. She needs someone to guide her. That someone is you.

For this short time, include her, kindly, into your life. Make her stay as comfortable as you can. Swallow your hurt feelings and share, even when you have to grit your teeth to do it. Ask God to change your feelings. He can! Then ask Him to fill the rest of your summer with such joy, peace, and happiness that it will make your

Chatting With Girls Like You

sacrifice worthwhile. You might find out you *like* clarinet music. Someday *you* will be the stranger. Try to treat your exchange student as you'd want someone to treat you. As a friend.

Have you ever had an exchange student, an extended family member, or someone not normally a part of your family live with you?

What is the hardest part of that? What is the best part?

Whom can you treat kindly, as if you were being kind to your Lord? (Because, really, you are. . . .)

> *I was alone and away from home, and you invited me into your house. . . . Then the good people will answer, "Lord . . . when did we see you alone and away from home and invite you into our house? . . ." Then the King will answer, "I tell you the truth. Anything you did for any of my people here, you also did for me."*
> MATTHEW 25:35, 37–38, 40

Friends

How do you know if someone is a true friend?

In this world everyone wants to "look out for number one," meaning themselves. It's hard to tell who is a true friend and who is a false friend. Smart girls like you start by considering a few friendship facts:

1. Not all friends need to be equal friends. Some friends are really "acquaintances," people we see from time to time, people we like but who really aren't involved in our lives. It's okay to have lots of acquaintances. In fact, if you try to make all of your acquaintances your friends, you soon won't have enough time for real friends!
2. Not all friends are good friends. Friends who try to control you, friends who boss you around, and friends who backstab you really aren't friends. Sometimes we know that in our hearts, but we don't want to face it. Don't be afraid to leave bad friendships. God will replace them with good friendships.
3. Real friends will allow you to put them first sometimes, but they will also put you first sometimes. Like a teeter-totter! Sometimes you're up when they are down. You give them a push, and for a while, you're balanced. Sometimes they're up when you're down. They'll give you a push, and then you're balanced for a while. Real friendships are equal friendships. They both help and allow you to help.

In the Bible, Job had many problems. His livestock and servants were stolen and burned—kind of like losing your whole business in a fire with no fire insurance. His house was destroyed. His children died. Job got very sick. He did have some friends, though. Now, his friends didn't do and say everything right. But they were good friends. They left their own homes and businesses to be with a friend who was sad and in trouble. They focused on Job when he was down and needed them. They comforted him. They stayed with him. Sometimes they reminded Job of God's goodness and power. When Job was down, they pushed him back up again! The Bible doesn't tell us if Job did the same for them, but his character showed that he honored God and others. That is a true friend.

Chatting With Girls Like You

What does true friendship mean to you?

Who is a true friend to you? Have you thanked her lately?

> *Now Job had three friends.... These friends heard about the troubles that had happened to Job. So they agreed to meet and go see Job. They wanted to show him they were upset for him, too. And they wanted to comfort him.*
> JOB 2:11

Friends

There's a new girl in my class. She still wears sneakers that light up, and her shirts are weird. My friends and I aren't sure what to do. She might be nice—but maybe not.

One day my family and I were at an outdoor festival. We were walking around, looking at the booths, tasting the food, listening to the music. I watched the people. I like to people-watch.

A man walked by me. He had tattoos all up and down his arms—kind of freaky-looking ones. His hair was chopped back. He had on black boots with studs on the side. As he walked by, his T-shirt caught my eye. It said, *Body piercing saved my life.* I thought, *What?* I had already decided in my heart this guy was scary and weird, but I turned around to look back at him. When I did, I caught the picture on the back of his T-shirt.

It was a picture of Jesus on the cross.

Jesus' hands and feet were pierced. Jesus' body piercing saved *my* life, too. I felt sad that I had made such a snappy judgment against a brother in Christ.

It's so easy to judge a person by the outside. We do it all the time. But the Bible teaches that life consists of far more than food and clothing. It is made up of what is inside a person's heart—her thoughts, her intentions, her deeds, her spirit. What is inside is much more important than what is outside.

Give the new girl a chance. You don't *have* to be friends with her. But before you make that decision, see what's on the inside. After all, we all know perfectly dressed people who are lemons inside.

What kind of clothes are easy for you to judge people by?

Chatting With Girls Like You

What's the best way you know of to determine if a person is worth choosing as a friend or not?

But the Lord said to Samuel, "Don't look at how handsome Eliab is. Don't look at how tall he is. I have not chosen him. God does not see the same way people see. People look at the outside of a person, but the Lord looks at the heart."
1 Samuel 16:7

Friends

There are some girls in my class who think they are so cool. Sometimes they will whisper secrets about other people. What should I do?

Sometimes quiet sounds make a bigger impact than loud noises. For example, the doctor can tell a pregnant woman that her baby is okay in a loud voice. When the mom hears the baby's heart beating through the stethoscope, though, gentle as the sound may be, it will be a more powerful reassurance than words. That's a good way to use a quiet noise. A bad way to use a quiet noise is gossip. That's really what quiet secrets are.

When people tell secrets, it's because they don't want anyone else to know what they are doing. Some secrets—better called surprises—are good. It might be a planned gift or party. Another appropriate secret might be something you want to share about yourself with a trusted friend but not with anyone else.

One kind of secret that is *not* okay is when something has harmed you or could harm someone else. If someone has hurt you physically, touched you in a wrong place, or has torn you down with his or her words, you need adult help. Those are secrets you must not keep. Please tell a trusted adult—a family member, a teacher, or a friend's parent. If someone you know plans to hurt someone else—either physically or even with words by spreading rumors or gossip—you need help then, too. Ask an adult to intervene. Why don't people want harmful things known? Because they know it's wrong. It's a weak way to hurt someone who can't protect herself.

What can you do? Keep a clean mouth. Girls like you might use this good rule of thumb when talking with friends: Talk about yourself, talk about the person or people you're with, talk about pets, or say anything kind or generous about anyone not present. That way you'll avoid gossip. If you happen to overhear these girls whispering, walk away. Someday soon the things they say will come to light. The friends who whisper with them will soon whisper about them. Don't be a part of any friendship group like that.

Chatting With Girls Like You

When are you tempted to gossip? (We all are. . . .)

What can you do to avoid gossip?

What will you do next time someone is whispering secrets and you're standing there, too?

> *The time is coming when everything will be revealed; all that is secret will be made public. Whatever you have said in the dark will be heard in the light, and what you have whispered behind closed doors will be shouted from the housetops for all to hear!*
> LUKE 12:2–3 NLT

Friends

If you are having a party and someone you didn't invite asks if you are having a party, what should you do? Also, should you invite only old, good friends to a party or new friends you are trying to get to know?

Thank you for having a sensitive heart! It shows what a caring girl you are that you're even thinking about these questions. I know girls who don't even have a birthday party because they don't want to invite certain people but are afraid of what will happen if they don't. Don't let fear run your life.

Honesty really *is* always the best policy. You need to understand in your own heart, first, that this party is *your* party, kind of like a gift to yourself. You are not required to invite anyone to your party that you don't want there. No one is entitled to come to your party—although some people may feel like they are. What you are required to do is be honest, kind, and considerate. Here's how: If someone asks you, "Are you having a party?" first, simply answer yes. Then try to change the subject. If that person persists and asks, "Why am I not invited?" you might try saying, "I couldn't invite everyone, but perhaps you and I could do something another time." Then change the subject. You will then have been honest, kind, and considerate. Understand her hurt feelings, and don't hold them against her or gossip, but don't give in, either.

I know it's hard to be direct, but life is full of peer pressure. Better to learn how to say yes and no right now! Anyone who is going to punish you for saying no politely is probably not a good friend, anyway. Paul tells us in 2 Corinthians 1 to make sure we say yes when we mean yes, no when we mean no, and to leave nothing between the lines. That means being straightforward with your thoughts and feelings. It's okay. He tells us why, too. Because that's how Jesus acted.

Whom should you invite? Old, good friends are always a good choice, but so are a couple of people you'd like to get to know better. Celebrating with old friends will make it special, and inviting

Chatting With Girls Like You

someone new to a party will be fun. It's not as personal as a one-on-one get-together, but it might be a good place to start a new friendship. Just remember—invite those people *you* want to celebrate with!

When is it hard for you to tell people no?

Can you prepare a response ahead of time and practice it, so when the sweaty-palms moment comes you'll be prepared?

Just say a simple yes or no, so that you will not sin and be condemned for it.
JAMES 5:12B NLT

Friends

What can I do if one friend wants to hog me all the time? She cries or gets mad or ignores me if I "dare" to have another friend. I went to a movie with other friends, but I don't want to tell my best friend because she'll be mad at me. Now I feel dishonest. What should I do?

There are two types of dishonesty—one is lying, which you have not done, and one is withholding necessary information, which you have not done. Be at peace. You haven't been dishonest. Your friend does not have a "right" to know where you are, and with whom, at all times. You don't owe her an explanation for your every move.

She's made you feel as though you owe her that. The people who have legitimate control over you need to know where you are, with whom, and for how long. You need to seek their permission. Who has legitimate control over you? Your parents, a grandparent in charge, or a daycare provider. Your school, during the school day. Sunday school teachers on Sunday or at a youth event. Not friends. Friends are to exercise *self*-control, not *other* control.

Your friend has made a condition on your friendship—you do things her way or she's not going to be your friend. Or she'll remain your friend but be very angry. That's controlling you. You don't feel free to be honest, to be yourself, because of that control. These kinds of friends generally are very nice and kind for a while. They can be fun to be around. But when you decide to do things your way and not their way, they make you "pay" emotionally. Your friend might not realize that she is doing this. You can be a good friend to her and gently let her know.

Tell your friend that while you enjoy her company, you also have other friends. Encourage her to do the same. If you can't be honest with her, how good can that friendship really be? A real friend is a 1 Corinthians 13 friend. Make sure you're one, too.

Chatting With Girls Like You

Do you have a friend or friends who punish you emotionally (ignoring you, leaving you out, getting angry with you) if you tell them no or do things your own way?

Would a real friend want to cut you off from all other friends, or would she encourage you to have other friends, too?

Do *you* try to control anyone by pouting, shouting, or gift giving?

> *Love is patient and kind. Love is not jealous, it does not brag, and it is not proud. Love is not rude, is not selfish, and does not become angry easily. Love does not remember wrongs done against it.*
> 1 Corinthians 13:4–5

Friends

What should you do if you get angry at a friend? What if my friend is mad at me? Are friends supposed to be angry with one another? It scares me.

The word *hypocrite* tastes bad in our mouths, doesn't it? It means two-faced, someone who does one thing and says another or pretends to be someone she isn't. None of us would want to think of ourselves as hypocrites. But we all are in some ways!

The word hypocrite comes from a Greek word that means *actor*. When the Greeks put on plays, the actors would hold masks in front of their faces. Even if they were sad inside, they'd hold up a happy mask. They did this to try to make the people around them think that they were happy. It might have worked for a little while. It wasn't honest, though. Inside, they were sad.

Being mad at someone is scary, because you don't know how they are going to react to your anger. Will they stop liking you? Stop being your friend? Will they be angry back? That's why we often pretend we're not angry when, really, we are. We put up that happy mask because we don't want to risk losing a friend. But inside we're still mad. We're holding on to that anger because we never work through it. Eventually, it will poison the friendship. Poisoned friendships usually die—just the thing you were hoping to avoid!

When you're angry with a friend, first let your emotions cool down some so you don't say something you'll regret later. Practice saying out loud what you'd like to tell your friend. Listen to your own voice and decide if it sounds like something you'd be okay hearing. Pray about it, and then talk with your friend. Chances are she won't even know that she's hurt you. Give her a chance to make things right. You'll want that same right next time you hurt her! Be ready to accept when you're wrong, too! If she doesn't like you when you take the mask off—if you do it in love and with gentleness—she wasn't a real friend anyway.

Chatting With Girls Like You

Whom are you afraid to show your anger toward? What response do you fear?

What will you do next time you're angry with that person?

So put away all falsehood and "tell your neighbor the truth" because we belong to each other. And "don't sin by letting anger gain control over you." Don't let the sun go down while you are still angry, for anger gives a mighty foothold to the Devil.
EPHESIANS 4:25–27 NLT

Friends

I have a really good friend who's a Christian, but she never acts like a Christian. She never takes the time to talk or to pray. She always says "Oh my God." How can I make her love and trust Jesus like I do?

How wonderful that you are interested in your friend and know her well enough to see her relationship with God! Good for you! You've asked an important question.

It's often been said that God is a gentleman. He doesn't force anyone to be His friend, His follower, or His servant. He invites us to do that, but we have to make the move. If you read through the Bible, you'll see that God makes an invitation and then waits for us to make a move. He says, "Come close to me and I will come close to you. Seek and you will find. Knock and it will be answered." He expects us to make a move. Your friend is no different.

As wonderful as you are, you can't "make" her be a Christian; she has to choose that. If she's already a Christian, she has to choose to spend time with God. There is something you *can* do, though. What? Set a great example. When my kids were little, they very often refused to eat food that I knew they would think tasted good. Instead of trying to force open their little (but very strong!) mouths and slip in a sliver of ham, I would eat my ham in front of them. I'd smack my lips, say "Mmm!" and generally show that I was having a good time. Because I was enjoying it, they wanted to try, too—by their choice, not force. (Both of them like ham now, by the way!)

Maybe your friend is a new Christian and hasn't had many good examples. Maybe she hasn't yet learned the things you have learned. Don't judge—instead, be a leader in your love and in your actions. Make sure your language stays pure, and when your friend asks for help, tell her you'll pray about it, and then do! Invite her to church outreaches and parties. Let her watch you and see your shining light. Maybe she'll see you enjoying your faith and want to try, too.

Chatting With Girls Like You

Do you have Christian friends for whom you'd like to set a good example?

What are some practical ways you can do that?

1.

2.

3.

Follow my example, as I follow the example of Christ.
1 CORINTHIANS 11:1

Part Two

Myself

Long ago the Lord said to Israel: "I have loved you, my people, with an everlasting love. With unfailing love I have drawn you to myself."

JEREMIAH 31:3 NLT

Girls Like You Wonder...

1. Why do I spend money too fast—and my best friend hardly spends hers at all?

2. I worry about what kind of person I'll be when I'm older. Is there any way to know?

3. Why did God make us have sad emotions?

4. What can I do if people are jealous of me?

5. I am tempted to swear. How should I handle it—is it ever okay?

6. Why are girls so different from boys? Is it inside as well as out?

7. I have an embarrassing problem. How can I stop being bossy to others?

8. I'm uncomfortable with changes in my body. Is everyone else?

9. Is it okay to act different around various people?

10. Is it okay for kids to get their ears double-pierced?

Myself

Whenever I get money, I want to spend it all. What can I do?

There are so many things in the world we live in—things to do, things to buy, places to go. It reminds me of a restaurant I once went to. There were 150 items on the menu. I had the hardest time deciding on just one thing to order—and then I wondered if I'd chosen well. I almost didn't go back to that restaurant. I don't like to have too many choices. It confuses me—or makes me overeat!

That's how it is when you get money. Suddenly you realize how many things you'd like, how many things you can buy. You might also realize that there are things you want that cost more than you have. You might have a heart to help people in need. Here's a system that might work.

First, get three containers. They might be plastic food-storage containers, sandwich bags, or baby food jars with lids. On one write, "Buy Now!" On the second write, "Buy Later!" On the third write, "God's Heart." From now on, whenever you get money, divide it between those three containers right away. Talk with your parents about how much to spend now, how much to save for something bigger, and how much to give in a way that honors God. Whenever you do that, you will get three different great feelings. One, you'll get the fun of having mad money, money you can spend however you want, right away. Even on junk! Second, you'll have the pleasure of looking forward to buying something you need to save for. You'll also have the satisfaction when you get it. Third, you'll have the joy and pleasure of giving something to God, by giving to the people He loves.

Chatting With Girls Like You

Do you have a good system to spend, save, and give? If not, when will you make one?

What changes happen in a person's heart when she spends everything on herself, right away?

What happens in a person's heart when she spends some, saves some, and gives some away?

The wise man saves for the future, but the foolish man spends whatever he gets.
PROVERBS 21:20 TLB

Myself

What kind of person will I be when I'm older?

I'm not a very good artist. I like to write, I like to take pictures, I like to scrapbook. But I can't draw very well. It's always been very embarrassing.

One day my daughter offered to show me how to sketch. Instead of putting down a pencil or pen and drawing one solid line that will become a picture, sketching involves using many short lines, made one at a time, in order to make a picture. At first when you're sketching, you can't see what it's going to be. It looks like funny hairs lying across the page instead of a picture! Sometimes lines are made in one place, then another, and aren't connected for quite a while. After they *are* connected, you can see a shape, but it isn't three-dimensional. Not yet lifelike. That comes after you shade—turn the pencil on its side and make the picture deeper. Finally it's done. What started out as a bunch of disconnected lines turns into a picture of great clarity and meaning. Each line is important to the whole. It may have seemed randomly placed, but it wasn't. The picture would not be complete without each of those individual sketches.

This is how your life is, especially now as a girl. You walk through your days making choices. What will I wear? How will I spend my time? Will I study my Bible and talk with God or not? Will I take care of my body? When I am offered the opportunity to do good, will I? If I'm tempted to cheat, will I? Each choice is a line that will connect with all of the other choices you make. Each choice may seem separate from other choices, but it's not. They all connect to make the woman you are becoming.

When you wake in the morning, pray and ask God to help you make good decisions that day. Be aware that, like an artist, you are shaping a woman out of the girl you are. The opportunities and life that woman will have depend in many ways on the choices the girl makes today.

Chatting With Girls Like You

What are three things you have done this week that will influence the kind of woman you will become?

1.

2.

3.

What one thing can you do today to begin to be more like the person you'd like to be when you're grown-up?

Happy is the person who doesn't listen to the wicked. He doesn't go where sinners go. He doesn't do what bad people do. He loves the Lord's teachings. He thinks about those teachings day and night. He is strong, like a tree planted by a river. It produces fruit in season. Its leaves don't die. Everything he does will succeed.
PSALMS 1:1–3

Myself

Why did God make us so we can cry?

When someone we love dies or our best friend decides she doesn't want to be friends anymore or our parents divorce or our cat runs away, it would seem better if we didn't have to feel sadness at all. Doesn't it? But then we have to think about *why* we are sad. Mostly we feel sad because first we feel love.

One year my family decided to buy one of those robotic pets. You know—the ones that work on batteries and will roll over or do tricks on command. They make purring sounds but are pretty cold. They don't have cuddly fur. They don't come for a pat on the head or an ear rub. They don't nuzzle you to see you jump. They don't sense when you're sad and lick your tears away. These pets don't love you, and you don't love them.

We got tired of the fake pet pretty soon and put it away. Strangely, no one cared. When we had to send our dog to live on a sheep farm where she'd be more happy, though, we all bawled our eyes out for a month. We loved her, which is why we sent her to be happy. If we hadn't loved, we couldn't feel loss. When we feel loss, we're sad. When people are sad, they cry.

God made us in His image. We don't know what God looks like; He is Spirit, after all. But we do know that He has emotions, because the Bible tells us that. Among other feelings, God himself feels love, anger, and sorrow. When Jesus was here on earth and He lost a friend, He cried.

None of us likes to cry for sadness. And sometimes even crying when we're happy can feel a little uncomfortable, though it's perfectly okay. But it'd be a whole lot worse to never love anyone or anything, feel neither sorrow nor joy. When we love, there will always be a loss. But that is *real* life, not robotic.

What has made you cry?

Chatting With Girls Like You

How does that involve love and then a loss?

*Jesus saw that Mary was crying and that the Jews who came with her were crying, too. Jesus felt very sad in his heart and was deeply troubled. He asked, "Where did you bury him?" "Come and see, Lord," they said.
Jesus cried.*
JOHN 11:33–35

Myself

What can I do if people are jealous of me?

Generally, people are jealous of others if they are insecure about themselves. To envy means to want something that someone else has. Sometimes it might be their stuff—you could envy someone's clothes, her house, or her friends. You want them for yourself because you don't have those things and think you'll be happy if you get them.

People can also be jealous about other people's personal qualities. Maybe someone is jealous of your ability to get good grades. Maybe you're jealous of someone else's ability to talk to others. People might be jealous if it seems that the popular kids like you or boys think you're cute. All of it is the same, though. People think they'll be happy if they get what you have.

The truth is, contentment comes from someplace inside us, not from anything outside of us. It comes with being satisfied with the way God made you. He might have made you tall or short. You might have blond hair or brown. You might be good in math but not in music, or good at writing but not at science. Everyone has some strong talents and some weaknesses. God can help you be content if you ask Him and then practice it.

You can't do anything to make other people be *not* jealous of you. Their emotions belong to them. Your actions and emotions belong to you, though. There are several things you *can* do. You can ask yourself, *Am I rubbing it in? Do I raise my hand every time I know the answer, to prove how smart I am? Do I make a big deal out of hanging out with my group of friends? Do I show off my stuff? Do I flirt in front of others?* Then, be sure to compliment others. The Bible says it is better for praise to come from the mouths of others than from your own mouth. That means not bragging on yourself and making sure you compliment others. Don't do it in a dishonest way, but look for things the people around you truly are good at, then tell them so.

Everything good about you comes from God. Therefore, there is nothing to brag about in yourself but also nothing to feel bad about if you have strengths that others do not. Examine your own

Chatting With Girls Like You

heart and your own motives. Help others feel good about their God-given gifts and talents so you win friends and not enemies.

How many times a day do you genuinely compliment someone else?

What strengths do you have? How do you know they come from God?

God, examine me and know my heart. Test me and know my thoughts. See if there is any bad thing in me. Lead me in the way you set long ago.
PSALM 139:23–24

Myself

I feel tempted to swear. Some of my friends do. What should I do?

It's very cool that you understand you are tempted—that you see it, that you're concerned, and that you want an answer. Good job! That's further along than many adults are. Girls like you are smart to recognize temptation and make a plan.

One thing that has helped me, when I see others doing things, is to remember: I live by standards, not by comparisons. What does that mean? It means I do or don't do something not because others are doing it (or not doing it) but because it fits in with the way I have decided to live my life. Since I try to live my life according to what God says is good, swearing would be out.

Our language identifies us with others. If we are Americans in Spain and we hear someone else speaking American English, we instantly feel a bond with that person. We have something in common! We belong together, somehow. When your friends swear, you might want to do it, too, to fit in with them. When others see you with them, though, they might assume you belong with the kids who swear. Kids and adults will associate you with that group whether you want them to or not.

The Bible tells us not to use bad language, only words that would be helpful and encouraging to others. If you were to swear, it would tell your friends that you think it's okay. If you don't think it's okay (and you don't, or you wouldn't have asked), you would be helping them to do wrong. You would not be helpful and encouraging. If your standard for life is to live as God wants, swearing is pretty much out.

Pray and ask the Lord to help you overcome your desire to swear. You can find other ways to identify with your friends. Maybe you all sit at a certain lunch table. You share CDs together. You call one another, and you remind one another about homework. These are ways that you can be similar and still be helpful to one another. When they choose bad language, remain silent. Your silence will be even more powerful than their bad language. If they continue to use bad language, you might need to choose other friends. If you

Chatting With Girls Like You

need to make poor choices in order to fit in with these friends, they aren't good friends. Ask God to provide some friends who make better choices. Then, when you do things together, those words and actions will be in line with your standards. Watch and see.

Do you feel tempted to make poor choices to fit in with your friends? Do these friends make more poor choices than good choices? What things do they do that agree with what the Bible says is good or what it says is bad?

Pray right now and ask God to show you which friends are "keepers" and which friends you might be better off without.

I did that.

_____
(Sign here)

But remember that the temptations that come into your life are no different from what others experience. And God is faithful. He will keep the temptation from becoming so strong that you can't stand up against it. When you are tempted, he will show you a way out so that you will not give in to it.
1 Corinthians 10:13 NLT

Myself

Why are girls so different from boys?

Our God is an endlessly creative God. He designed all of the plants, all animals, even all of the natural laws. For example, He designed the way the moon's cycles work and direct the ocean tides. Seasons, as He created them, allow the land to rest, to produce, then to rest again. Everything God created displays His individuality, shows His tender care, and is designed with His purposes in mind.

The Bible tells us that God created men and women. Men and women are both created in God's image. They are equally valuable to Him. But, like everything else God created, they each have slightly different purposes. Men's bodies are formed to father children. Women's bodies are formed to mother children. While mothers and fathers are both important, they are not the same. Both men and women are relational, but women typically enjoy and need relationships more. While both women and men are competitive, men are typically more so. These strengths allow men and women to better do the tasks He has set aside for them to do.

Today, some people try to make boys and girls out to be the same. They think that if boys and girls are given the same opportunities and told the same things, they will come out the same. This is not true. Even when boys and girls are given the same opportunities, they often freely choose to be involved with different things and approach life differently. God did not make boys and girls the same, and being free to act as a boy if you're a boy and as a girl if you're a girl is true freedom and equality.

God's laws are unchangeable. Seasons do not vary, no matter how we try to manipulate them. When we work with the strengths He gave us, and not against them, we find success. Who plants in wintertime and expects a good crop? In the same way, we should not expect men to act as women or women to act as men.

Be honored to be a girl like you, a woman. In the same way, honor your brothers and other boys, too, in the ways that they are different from you. Someday you may find that one of those boys

Chatting With Girls Like You

grows up to be a man who perfectly complements the woman you are, and together, you'll be one.

What differences do you see between boys and girls?

How is your dad different from your mom?

Do you generally tolerate boys and their differentness, or do they irritate you?

> *So God created human beings in his image. In the image of God he created them. He created them male and female.*
> GENESIS 1:27

Myself

How can I stop being bossy to others?

You're a wise girl to see this in yourself or to have listened when someone else told you that you were bossy. That's part of the battle. Now, if you can understand why you boss and then change your actions, you'll be all the way there. Way to go!

People boss others when they want their own way all the time. Sometimes this happens because a girl feels like she always needs to be in control. She feels scared that she will be left out or ignored if she isn't in control. By controlling others, she thinks, she'll keep them close to her. The opposite usually happens. People get so smothered from the bossing, they run away.

Sometimes girls boss people because they feel that their way is best. They don't see that, in many cases, there are lots of different ways to do or say things. Other girls have good ideas, too. It can be hard for someone who is tempted to boss to even realize that others have good ideas. You might have to just trust that they do until you really see that they do.

When you let others choose what to do or what to say, you are giving them honor. You're telling them that you value their ideas, their thoughts, and their conversation. If you're always in charge, you're really telling them that they must always honor you. I know that's not what you mean! When you let others choose you to play or come along, rather than your always controlling it, it's really better. Why? Because you're allowing them to show you love, to pick you rather than be forced to be with you. Having someone choose you is always better.

Next time you're tempted to tell others what to do, keep quiet. It will be hard, and it will take practice. Allow others to do things their way till they ask you if you have an idea. Then you can share! Allow others to plan things and include you. When they do—and they will if you give it time—you'll feel real love. You won't be controlling them, and they will choose you.

Chatting With Girls Like You

Are you always the boss in your group of friends? Do others get to share and do their ideas?

What are three areas, either people or situations, that you try to control?

1.

2.

3.

How can you stop trying to control them?

Your love must be real. . . . Give your brothers and sisters more honor than you want for yourselves.
ROMANS 12:9–10

Myself

My breasts are growing and it feels uncomfortable. What can I do?

Have you ever wondered how a giant oak tree can grow from a tiny acorn? The acorn shell is so hard. How does the plant burst out? In the same way, your body grows from a tiny body at birth to the larger body you will have when you're a fully grown woman. One of the truths about growth of any kind is it can hurt!

When I was a girl your age, I woke up almost every night with growing pains in my legs. My bones were stretching, and they grew while I was at rest, which was at night. The alternative—not growing at all—was not an option! So I took some medicine when I needed to, and hot baths, and wore comfy jammies. In a few years my legs were as long as they were going to get and they stopped hurting.

Your breasts are growing from those of a young girl into those of a woman. The same hormones that cause them to grow can also cause them to feel tender. Wearing a well-fitting bra that keeps your breasts closer to your body will help. Recognizing that the pain may come and go in monthly cycles will help, too. Part of the discomfort might be emotional. You feel differently about your body as it becomes a woman's body. You might draw more attention. You're not used to looking that way. All of that is uncomfortable. But it's all normal, too. It's the way your body was designed to be. God designed your body with the greatest care. Of all of His creations, humans are most important to Him. The growth that you are experiencing was all planned by Him, and He plans only for your good.

Be gentle with yourself. Talk with your mom or an aunt about your feelings as your body grows. Wear comfy clothes that make you feel good about yourself. Most of all, be proud that you're becoming a woman. Read a helpful book like *A Growing-Up Guide* (written by me!) and learn more about the what, why, when, and how of growing up. Then enjoy. It's who God designed you to be!

Chatting With Girls Like You

What part about growing up is uncomfortable—either physically or emotionally—right now?

With whom have you talked about this? Will you talk with someone soon? Who? When?

We, out of all creation, became his choice possession.
JAMES 1:18B NLT

Myself

Is it okay to be quiet around some people and hyper around others?

One of the most important qualities in any Christian is honesty. That means we say what we mean. We aren't kind to some people and not to others. We are gentle to both our friends and those we don't really care for. That doesn't mean, however, that you have to share your lives equally with all people.

God created you with a unique personality. You will have likes and dislikes, and so do others. When you have those things in common with others, you will often be friends. If you like softball and so does someone else, if you both read the same kinds of books and hate history, you'll probably be friends. When you're friends with someone, you'll find it easier to talk with them. If you have little in common with others, you'll have less to talk about. Sometimes our friends mean different things to us. A friend on a sports team might bring out a competitive nature in you. A friend who loves to talk may spend hours chatting with you on the phone. A zany friend can free you to be zany, too!

A girl like you, who wants to be like Jesus, still has some requirements. You must be kind to all. You must be gentle. You must be honest. I once read the best illustration for this: If you squeeze a tube of toothpaste, what's going to come out? Toothpaste! Whatever is inside you is what is going to come out in your words and your deeds. You might want gel candy to come out, but if toothpaste is inside of you, that's what's going to come out. Jesus said that whatever is in a man's heart comes out of his mouth. The more time you spend with God, the more you allow the Holy Spirit to direct you, the more fruit of His spirit you'll show.

It's okay to be more comfortable with some people than others. In fact, it's wise! Just make sure that what's inside you is juicy fruit and that whatever you do share with others is sweet.

Chatting With Girls Like You

Who are five people you are comfortable with?

1.

2.

3.

4.

5.

What are two things you can do that will allow God to have more control over your life?

1.

2.

> *But when the Holy Spirit controls our lives, he will produce this kind of fruit in us: love, joy, peace, patience, kindness, goodness, faithfulness, gentleness, and self-control. Here there is no conflict with the law.*
> GALATIANS 5:22–23 NLT

Myself

Why won't my mom let me get my ears double-pierced?

Your parents have an awesome responsibility. They have to explain to God why they made the choices they made as your parents. They love you very much. They want to do everything they can to make sure you grow up happy and healthy. They want you to be the best young lady you can be. It's not always easy to figure out how to do that!

Have you ever done those pencil mazes? You start from one side and then try to find your way out. Along the way you might take a wrong turn, but then you go back and retrace to the place you went wrong. If you take a wrong path, you may find your way out of the maze, but it won't be the exact place you wanted to end up.

Your parents are walking through a maze with you. They are making choices for and with you every day. They want those choices to help you end up in a good place. They are raising you to be a godly young woman. Sometimes they make decisions you don't agree with. Sometimes they might even make mistakes. When they do, good parents turn around, backtrack, and start over. Why are they willing to do this? Because they want you to come out right! They know if they show you the right path now, you're going to stay on that path later, too.

Smart girls like you try hard to be patient with the decisions their parents make for them, even if you don't agree. Almost everything they do, they do because they love you. When you end up a beautiful, Christlike woman, you can thank them. You can double-pierce your ears, if you still want to, when you're an adult!

Chatting With Girls Like You

What decisions have your parents made for you that you don't agree with?

Have you asked them why they made those choices? What did they say?

Train a child how to live the right way. Then even when he is old, he will still live that way.
PROVERBS 22:6

Part Three

Faith

This Good News tells us how God makes us right in his sight. This is accomplished from start to finish by faith. As the Scriptures say, "It is through faith that a righteous person has life."
ROMANS 1:17 NLT

Girls Like You Wonder...

1. The Bible confuses me. Am I weird or a bad Christian?

2. Why do some people lift their hands in church?

3. Why did Jesus love kids so much?

4. Are there really evil spirits and demons?

5. If it's so bad, why did God allow people to sin in the first place?

6. I know I should, but why are we supposed to get baptized?

7. What is speaking in tongues? Am I supposed to do that?

8. Why does God test us?

9. Will my dog go to heaven?

10. How do you know heaven is real? What if I'm not sure that I want to go there?

Faith

I've tried reading the Bible, but it's confusing. If God wanted me to read it, why is it hard to understand?

One of the most wonderful things about God is that He cares about talking directly to *you*! It's so exciting when you get a letter in the mail with a different stamp or pretty stationery or a whiff of perfume sprayed inside. It says *I care!* If you speak only English, your family and friends won't write to you in French. They'll write to you in English because they want you to understand what they have to say. When someone writes to you, she takes time to talk to you personally; she thinks you are important. If you don't understand what she's saying, you can ask her to explain and she will!

God thinks you are important, too. He wants you to understand the things He had written in the Bible, His personal letter to you. It helps if you read a version that sounds like the language you speak rather than one with funny-sounding phrases or outdated language. Translations such as the New Living Translation or the International Children's Bible read just like you talk. Don't just pick and choose little parts to read—choose a book of the Bible and read it through from beginning to end. How much of a letter or other books would you understand if you read only a few sentences here and there?!

The Bible isn't an instant message, something to be quickly read and easily understood. It takes time and attention and quiet. You have to focus, as if you were lip-reading. Keep your attention on God, and He will make things clear. If, after getting an easier translation and setting aside quiet time in your day and in your heart to listen, you still don't understand, ask for help. The book of 2 Peter tells us there are parts of the Bible that are hard to understand. You can ask God to guide you in your understanding, and He will. The book of 2 Corinthians promises that the Holy Spirit will show us God's deep secrets and help us understand. Sometimes God will make the meaning clear in your heart. Sometimes He will use someone else to show you. He is faithful to help you understand what He wants you to know.

Chatting With Girls Like You

How often do you read your Bible, compared with instant messages, emails, or other books?

Whom can you ask for help in understanding what God has to say to you in His Word?

Open my eyes to see the wonderful truths in your law.
Psalm 119:18 NLT

Faith

Why do people sometimes lift their hands in church?

Have you ever been to a play, concert, or ice-skating show? The performers all do their part, and then at the end they make a final appearance on the stage. One by one they come, from the least important player to, finally, the most important. As each actor comes onto the stage, she casts her hands up and out to welcome the next highest—and more important—level of actors. Finally, at the end, all performers hold their hands in the direction of the most important performer, player, or athlete. When they hold their hands toward the star, it brings glory and praise to that person. They recognize who deserves the highest honor.

So, too, when we lift our hands toward God, we are giving Him the honor, the glory, and the praise due to Him as the ultimate Star of the universe. We are praising Him for His work and His love. We hold our hands up to Him, open, as if to say, "We bring nothing to you but our love and devotion, but we offer that to you." We raise our hands at the mention of His name to show the respect due to His name. The Bible tells us to raise our hands to pray from the heart, to praise Him, to bless Him, and to show that we are holy, too. We draw all attention His way. It's a way to praise the Lord and to bless Him as He blesses us. You don't have to raise your hands to praise Him, of course. You can think of other ways to do that, too.

Do you feel comfortable raising a palm or arm or both in church? If so, do you focus on praising the Lord then? If not, can you show Him honor in other ways? How?

Chatting With Girls Like You

What does it mean to bless the Lord or praise Him?

Lift your hands in holiness, and bless the Lord.
PSALM 134:2 NLT

Faith

Why did Jesus love children so much?

Have you ever been in a home where a toddler lives? People take care not to drop pennies or small objects—they don't want the baby to put such things in her mouth and choke. They put locks on toilets so little children can't fall in and drown. They lock cupboards where poisons are stored to keep curious kids safe. When there are people around us who need special care or looking out for, we naturally tend to look out for them more.

The Bible tells us that God places great importance on taking care of people who need extra help. Maybe they don't have a dad. Maybe they don't have a husband or money. Maybe they're kids. Jesus himself warns that a terrible death would be better than the judgment that waits for people who lead children astray. He also tells us that the angels that protect children are always in God's presence—a place of instant access. Kids are important. They have important things to teach adults here on earth, too.

Girls like you get used to learning from adults. Jesus says adults can learn from kids, too. The kind of faith that kids have is the faith Jesus is looking for. Just like a toddler trusts that her parent will catch her if she jumps into deep water, so, too, do most kids trust God to catch them wherever life leads. Kids talk openly and honestly with Jesus. They usually aren't ashamed of His name. They run toward Jesus. They are often humble. That's the kind of faith you can model for the adults around you. You can be a good teacher, too.

Who around you needs your protection? Who in your life protects you?

Chatting With Girls Like You

How do you feel protecting others? When you are protected?

Can you be a good example for adult Christians by being humble, honest, open, and trusting of Jesus?

Therefore, anyone who becomes as humble as this little child is the greatest in the Kingdom of Heaven.
MATTHEW 18:4 NLT

Faith

Are there really evil spirits?

Yes. How do we know for sure? Because Jesus tells us in Matthew 10:1 and in other places, too.

The name Satan is a Hebrew word that means *enemy*, one who goes against you. Satan is the chief evil spirit, the enemy of God. Anyone who is God's enemy is your enemy, too. Satan hates you because you love God and God loves you. Those who obey Satan, evil spirits, are also your enemies. They can tempt you to do wrong or try to take advantage of your weaknesses. They can accuse you or lie to you. They try to make bad look good and good look bad. Enemies fight against us and want us to lose and be hurt.

Jesus tells us, though, that He has already won the fight against this world's evil. So even though Satan and his evil spirits (demons) can make a lot of noise, Jesus is already the winner. You are, too, if you are a Christian. A Christian is someone who recognizes that Jesus is God, acknowledges that He died on the cross for her sins, and trusts in Jesus as her Savior. The Holy Spirit lives in you, and because He is God, He is stronger than any evil you face.

Jesus also tells us that nothing can take us away from Him or His care. You are always protected.

Are you afraid of evil spirits? If so, whom can you talk to about this?

What (Who) protects you? Can anything separate you from God's love?

Chatting With Girls Like You

And I am convinced that nothing can ever separate us from his love. Death can't, and life can't. The angels can't, and the demons can't. Our fears for today, our worries about tomorrow, and even the powers of hell can't keep God's love away. Whether we are high above the sky or in the deepest ocean, nothing in all creation will ever be able to separate us from the love of God that is revealed in Christ Jesus our Lord.
ROMANS 8:38–39 NLT

Faith

God knew Adam and Eve would eat the fruit, so why did He put the tree in the garden?

God is the Creator of everything. He made all the trees, plants, animals, planets, stars, angels, and human beings. Most of His creation has no personal relationship with Him—that is, they can't interact. God can create trees, and He can enjoy their beauty, but trees don't love God back. Only angels and human beings are able to love God back.

You know how you feel about special stuffed animals or dolls? You love them, you care for them, you make sure they sit in a soft place on your bed. Even the most tender stuffed animal can't love you back, though, as much as you may want it to. I always wanted my doll to come alive and love me. She couldn't. People could, though. That is why, as much as I loved my dolls, I didn't love them as much as my best friends, my parents, or my brother and sister. My brother and I may have fought, but when he made a homemade card for me, he showed me how much he loved me. My doll never fought with me, but she never made a card for me, either.

When God created angels and humans, he wanted beings that could love Him back and choose to worship and obey Him. In order to do that, He had to give them a choice. They could choose to love and obey Him, or not. They could choose to fight against Him, but they could also make Him homemade cards or sing songs to Him. By putting the tree in the garden, God gave them the opportunity to obey Him—or not. If there was no way to sin, they could never make a free choice. As you know, they chose to disobey when they ate the fruit, but there were other times when they obeyed. Adam and Eve had the same choice we have every day—to obey God, or not. Sometimes we choose to obey, sometimes we choose not to. Love isn't really love unless the person has a choice to love or not. God wanted love, so He allows people to make choices for or against Him every day. Adam and Eve had the choice to obey and follow God or to choose sin. You have that choice, too.

Chatting With Girls Like You

How do you choose to show God your love in your everyday life?

When you make a choice to sin, do you repent, ask forgiveness, and begin again?

> *Don't you realize that whatever you choose to obey becomes your master? You can choose sin, which leads to death, or you can choose to obey God and receive his approval.*
> ROMANS 6:16 NLT

Faith

Why do people get baptized?

When I got married, I stood before a hundred people who knew me and my husband, and I said important things. I said that I would love and honor my husband-to-be and that I would not be interested in any other men from then on. I would be set aside only for him. My old single life was over—my married life was now beginning.

My husband said that he would love and take care of me and would not be interested in any other women from then on. He would be set aside only for me.

Everyone in the room heard us make those promises. When the going gets tough and I'm angry with my husband or he is angry with me, we remember those vows and we keep them.

In the same way, when you are baptized in front of people, you are telling them that your old life as a non-Christian is over and your new life as a Christian is beginning. You make a statement in front of all of the people there and in front of God that you are beginning a new life, making promises to live as a Christian, even when you're mad or angry or confused. It's a public promise, a public celebration, and the way to show just what is most important in your life. Some people are baptized as babies—if so, their parents promise to raise them as Christians until the babies grow into people old enough to make their own decision for Christ.

Because baptism is so important, Jesus commanded His disciples to baptize other believers. Baptism is one way to honor Him and show others around you whom your life is centered on.

Have you been baptized? If not, would you like to be?

Chatting With Girls Like You

What would baptism show all those around you?

Therefore, go and make disciples of all the nations, baptizing them in the name of the Father and the Son and the Holy Spirit.
MATTHEW 28:19 NLT

Faith

What is speaking in tongues? Am I supposed to do that?

Speaking in tongues is one of the many spiritual gifts the Lord may choose to give a Christian. The Bible tells us that there is a great variety of spiritual gifts and that the Holy Spirit is the one who gives them to Christians.

Imagine that you are a gardener and you want to grow a lovely, large garden with many healthy plants. You have a big toolbox and many people to assist you with your garden. You open your toolbox and begin to hand out tools. To some you may give shovels to till the soil and to dig holes. To others you might hand rakes, seeds, a hose, or some plant food. To others you might give stakes that hold up the growing plants. To some you will hand a chart that tells when and how to harvest. Each person is given the tool that the gardener wants him or her to use as they all work together to help grow a beautiful, fruitful garden. No tool is most important—the garden needs all of them. The gardener selects just the right gift, or tool, for each helper.

In the same way God gives spiritual gifts to Christians. First Corinthians 12 tells us that the gifts are chosen by Him and are to be used to help other Christians. The spiritual gifts include things like wisdom, discernment, the ability to teach, and speaking in tongues. Tongues is both a special prayer language, seen in 1 Corinthians 14:14, and also a humanly known/used language, seen in Acts 2. First Corinthians 14:27–28 is very clear that "if anyone speaks in a tongue, two—or at the most three—should speak, one at a time, and someone must interpret. If there is no interpreter, the speaker should keep quiet in the church and speak to himself and God" (NIV).

Are you supposed to speak in tongues? Only if God has given you that gift. If not, then you are supposed to use the ones He gave you. No matter what spiritual gifts God gives you, the Bible instructs us to desire the gifts that are most helpful to others. Be responsible to use what you're given to help His garden grow!

Chatting With Girls Like You

Where could you offer your time, your gifts, and your talents to help God's people?

Make a commitment to do so:

God has given gifts to each of you from his great variety of spiritual gifts. Manage them well so that God's generosity can flow through you.
1 PETER 4:10 NLT

Faith

Why does God test us?

Pop quiz. State-required testing. Pass or fail. Grades. All of those words can make your teeth ache, can't they? There's something about testing that makes us nervous. We're finding out what we know—and what we don't know.

If we use test results to tell us if we're good or bad people, we're going to be in *big* trouble for life. Tests come every day, and most of them have nothing to do with school. *Will I say something I will regret later? Should I give the money back? A little gossip won't hurt, right?* What tests show us is where we are weak and where we are strong. The strong areas are no sweat. You don't worry about 1 + 1 anymore, do you? In fact, you could probably teach a preschooler some easy math. Multiplying decimals, however, is probably a different story. You're still learning. Someday you'll master it. Till then, it's best to know where the holes are and get help to understand.

God allows tests to come to girls like you. Sometimes we pass with no problem. (I gave the money back!) Sometimes we fail. (I bad-mouthed that girl I'm angry with.) God tells us "Well done!" when we pass and "Try again" when we don't. When we're tested, we see where we're weak. When they make airliners, they test the metal to make sure it's all strong before it goes on the plane. If a part of the metal is weak, and it often is, the engineers take the time to strengthen it before it flies. Aren't you glad they do that? In the same way, God tests you and then takes the time (if you're willing) to strengthen your weak parts. He wants to use you, but He makes sure you're ready first. In everything we do, our goal is to be more like Jesus. That means letting God point out the weak parts and getting help to make them strong.

What character tests do you face?

Chatting With Girls Like You

What and who can help you get strong enough to pass those tests as easily as 1 + 1?

These trials are only to test your faith, to show that it is strong and pure. It is being tested as fire tests and purifies gold—and your faith is far more precious to God than mere gold.
1 Peter 1:7a NLT

Faith

Do animals really go to heaven?

The Bible doesn't specifically say if animals go to heaven or not. It would be easier for those of us who love animals if it did! But there are several things we do know:

1. God cares for animals. He created them and took special care in designing each animal with its own special features, strengths, and beauty. Genesis 1:22 says that God not only created birds and everything in the sea, but He also blessed them.
2. God watches His animals. Matthew 10:29 tells us that not even a sparrow falls to the ground without God knowing about it.
3. God created animals, but He created human beings to be more important than animals. He tells us that humans alone are created in His image. He tells human beings to rule over the animals, fish, and birds.
4. In heaven there will be no unhappiness, whether pets are there or not. We don't understand how that happens, but we trust that He is true to His word.

Do you help care for animals? If you have pets, do you show them love and give them time?

If you don't have any pets, can you make bird feeders or care for neighborhood pets?

Chatting With Girls Like You

Why are people more important than animals?

Lord, you protect both men and animals. God, your love is so precious!
PSALM 36:6C–7A

Faith

How do you know heaven is real? And what if I want to stay here instead? Is that normal?

The Bible talks about heaven more than five hundred times. If God says something once, it's important. If He mentions something five hundred times, He really wants you to pay attention. Jesus himself says He is preparing a place for us to be after our lives on this earth are over.

Imagine if you were having a houseguest, someone you really loved. You'd prepare the nicest guest room you had. Maybe you'd put some fresh flowers in it or a couple of candy bars for late-night snacks. My grandma used to love the candy bar Nut Goodies, so whenever she came to stay we made sure there were plenty of Nut Goodies around. We put fresh sheets on the bed and fluffed the pillows. Our nicest towels were laid out. The window was opened to let in a fresh breeze. We prepare a wonderful place for the person we're expecting. The Bible tells us that everything good comes from God; He is the source of good things. So what kind of wonderful place do you think He'll prepare for you? My grandma is in heaven right now. I wonder if she's got Nut Goodies!

As for staying here, it's good that you like the life you have. God means for us to enjoy this life. But when this life is over, don't be afraid to move forward into heaven. If you have received Christ as your Savior, heaven awaits you. An unborn baby thinks that living inside her mother is nice—warm, comfortable, quiet—and probably wouldn't choose to be born if given the choice. But now, living on the outside, would any of us choose to go back? No! In the same way, it can be scary for us to pass from this life to heaven, but I'll bet that once there, none of us will choose to go back!

Do you know for certain that you are going to heaven? If you don't know if you've received Christ as your Lord and Savior, ask the person who gave you this book to talk with you about it, or pray something like this:

Hello, Jesus. I'm not used to talking with you, but I'd like to. I'm not sure if I am going to heaven, but I want to. I'd also like to have

Chatting With Girls Like You

your friendship while I am here on earth. I'm sorry for everything I have done wrong. Will you please forgive me? I believe that you died to pay for all the wrong things I have done. Thank you. Will you please be in charge of my life from now on?

Congratulations! You have now trusted in Jesus Christ for your salvation.

What kinds of things would you do to prepare for a much-loved guest coming to stay with you?

Do you believe that the Lord is preparing somewhere special just for you?

There are many rooms in my Father's home, and I am going to prepare a place for you. If this were not so, I would tell you plainly. When everything is ready, I will come and get you, so that you will always be with me where I am.

JOHN 14:2–3 NLT

Part Four

Family

But as for me and my family, we will serve the Lord.
Joshua 24:15d NLT

Girls Like You Wonder...

1. I fight with my siblings all the time. Is this normal?

2. I have way too many chores to do. How can I get out of them?

3. Is it really okay if grandparents spoil you?

4. If my parents are divorced, does that mean I will be, too, when I grow up?

5. Why do people have to die?

6. Do you *always* have to do what your parents want you to do?

7. Do you always have to go to church?

8. What if a relative gives me a gift I don't want? Do I keep it and act fake?

9. My sister ignores me now. It kind of hurts, but I also feel tempted to ignore my little brother because he's a pain. Is all that okay?

10. My parents are too strict about my talking to boys. What can I do?

Family

My brother and I just can't get along. Seriously. What should we do?

When God created us, He put us into bodies and then into families. We have a physical family: mom and dad, brothers and sisters; and also a spiritual family: other Christians. God expects us to get along with both families.

Can't means you are not able. For example, I can't be a boy because I'm a girl. I can't wear pants that are thirty-six inches long without tripping or ripping them because I'm not tall enough. There is nothing I can do to change those facts. *Won't* is a word that means unwilling. *I won't clean my room, although I can, because I'm unwilling. I won't be kind because she's not kind to me. I'm unwilling.* It's hard to take, but you probably "won't" get along with your brother, rather than "can't." Unless your brother is abusing you, in which case you need adult help right away, getting along means both of you making that choice.

It's not going to be easy. James 4 tells us that fights and arguments come from selfish desires—putting your own wants first. Let your brother take the first turn or sit where he wants in the car. Stay out of his room. Don't give in when he picks a fight. Do something generous for him, expecting nothing in return. If he's hurtful, rather than hurting him back, ask your mom or dad to help you solve things in the right way. The amazing thing about living this way—a biblical way—is that it may not change your brother (though it may!) but it will certainly change you. For the better.

What is one good thing you can do for a brother or sister?

Chatting With Girls Like You

What gentle response can you have prepared in advance, ready to say the next time your brother or sister irritates you?

Who can help you if it's beyond your ability to fix on your own?

*A gentle answer turns away wrath,
but harsh words stir up anger.*
PROVERBS 15:1 NLT

Family

Why do we have to do chores all the time?

Part of being in a family is sharing responsibilities for what the family needs done. Take a soccer team, for example. You need to have several forwards to push the ball toward the opposite goal, several people in defense to guard your goal, and a goalie who guards the net. You need a team to get this done. One person alone cannot score, defend the field, and guard the goal. A team of one will be overwhelmed and lose.

Your family is a team. There are many things that need to be done. Parents need to work, pay bills, keep up the yard, and do housework. They have to arrange for schooling, music lessons, and sports for you. Their most important task is to help you learn to know and love Jesus. In order to help your team win, your parents need the rest of the family—kids—to help with those tasks.

Chores aren't fun. They're not fun for parents, and they're not fun for kids. But not everything that is good for you is fun. Sometimes it can just be rewarding. If you learn to take pleasure in a job well done as well as happiness in fun things, you will live a fulfilled life. Satisfaction with yourself is something that is earned—like a paycheck—and comes from pulling for and helping your team without complaining or arguing. God tells us in Philippians 2:13–14 that He'll help us to want to do what pleases Him and that He'll give us the power to do it.

What is your typical facial expression when you're asked to do a chore that you don't want to do?

What is your typical verbal response?

Chatting With Girls Like You

Are you sharing the load with your family team, or are you adding to the team's discontent? How can you be a positive influence in your family with chores?

> *Work hard and become a leader;*
> *be lazy and become a slave.*
> PROVERBS 12:24 NLT

Family

Is it okay if grandparents spoil you, or will it cause problems?

Being a parent is hard work. Parents love their kids, but they must enforce rules. It's your mom and dad's job to raise you to be healthy and godly, not always make you happy. I'm sure you've figured that out by now. It costs a lot of money to raise children—one study estimated it's almost $235,000 per kid. Wow! That means parents must work hard, and a lot of the money has to go for "needs" and not "wants."

The responsibilities of grandparents are different from those of parents. The Bible says that the older men and women are to set a good example for younger men and women. Your grandparents should support your parents in what they do—to help when they can, share wisdom, and give love. They also have more time—and often money—to spend on you! Many times they will have a listening ear and a ready hug because they need not discipline you. They may have money to spend on fun things like vacations or a ball game or an unexpected outfit. They can do and say things to let you know just how special you are with no expectations in return! It's pleasant for them to see the children of their own grown children.

As long as your grandparents respect and support the rules and patterns set down by your parents, you're not being spoiled—you're being loved! Be sure to be thankful, not expecting these extras, but enjoying them as they are freely given.

What are three nice things your grandparents do for you?

1.

2.

3.

Chatting With Girls Like You

Have you written your grandparents a thank-you note (not just talked to them by phone or on email) lately? When will you do so?

Grandchildren are the crowning glory of the aged.
PROVERBS 17:6A NLT

Family

If your parents break up, does that mean that you will, too, when you get married?

Divorce is hard. In the book of Malachi, the Bible says that God hates divorce. I'll bet that if you ask anyone who has ever been involved in a divorce—man, woman, or child—they would say that they hate divorce, too. All people marry with the intention of staying together.

Because our world isn't heaven, it is full of both health and sickness, purity and sin, giving and selfishness. We all struggle to make right decisions. Some of the choices people make hurt their spouse so much that the hurt person rightfully asks for a divorce. Other people make wrong decisions to divorce. Some people are divorced when they don't want to be. Most of the time it's a complicated situation.

Most parents want their kids to grow up to be wiser, stronger, godlier, and happier than they are. Because of this, your parents will not want you to undergo the pain of a divorce, even if they are divorced themselves. Reassure your parents of your love, and then ask them, "What can I do to avoid a divorce?" Although it might be painful for them to hear this question, your mom and dad will be glad that you eventually want to make the strongest marriage choice possible. They will share their experiences in this area with you so that you can make the best choices possible. Just because your parents divorced doesn't mean you will. You can learn from their experiences. You can keep your eyes on the Lord. You can get Christian counsel. God can take something that was painful for your parents and your family and use it to protect you and prepare your future. He can give you skills and insight that perhaps they didn't have.

No matter if your parents are divorced or not, ask them: What kinds of things can I do to have a healthy marriage when I grow up?

Chatting With Girls Like You

Are you willing to show respect and love to both of your parents and to any stepparents, no matter if they've made a decision to divorce or not?

And we know that God causes everything to work together for the good of those who love God and are called according to his purpose for them.
ROMANS 8:28 NLT

Family

Why did my grandpa have to die?

My grandpa was so fun. He would let me pretend to drive the car when it was parked in the driveway—and even use the steering wheel! He cooked with me and loved football and was really fun to watch TV with. He was also the first important person in my life who died. I felt empty and sad, probably like you do.

Everything God created on earth has a life cycle. Plants start out as seeds, become shoots, then plants, bear fruit with seeds, and wither away. Even nonliving things, such as cars and computers, work well for a time, then eventually break down and don't work well any longer. This book will eventually turn yellow and fade, then crumble away. Stars are born—and die. Every thing, and every person, has a time to be young, to be fresh, and to be energized, but then everything and everyone eventually grows older and tired. At some point people's bodies wear out, and they die.

The good news is God created humans to have a spirit that lives on after the body dies. Ecclesiastes 12:7 says that when the human body dies, the spirit inside returns to God, who made it. Plants decay back into the soil, computers and cars are crushed and recycled, books fade away, and bodies die, but human spirits live on.

How does it feel when someone you love dies? Does it make you feel any better to know that his or her spirit, the "real" person, lives on?

Chatting With Girls Like You

Knowing that you have a limited amount of time on earth, what are some things you'd like to make sure you do or become before your spirit returns to "report" to God?

> *There is a right time for everything.*
> *Everything on earth has its special season.*
> *There is a time to be born and a time to die.*
> ECCLESIASTES 3:1–2A

Family

Do I always have to do what my parents want me to do?

Remember the story of Queen Esther? She married a king named Xerxes. Xerxes had another queen first, but that queen did not honor him or his requests, so he sent her away and probably had her killed! The law of the land was that everyone, even the king's wife, must honor him and do as he asked. When it came time for the king to choose another wife, he chose Esther. Esther was beautiful and kind and godly. But even though Esther was queen, she knew that she must respect the rules of those in authority over her. That would be the king, who was also her husband.

Because of the schemes of an evil man, all of the Jews in Xerxes' kingdom were to be killed. The Jews begged Esther, who was also a Jew, to go to the king and save them. Because Esther had shown honor and respect to her husband and his rules, he was willing to listen to her request. She asked what she wanted and saved the Jews of the kingdom from death.

So what's the point here? Dishonor and get sent away to be killed? Respect your parents and become a queen? No! The lesson is, show respect for those in authority over you and live your life showing honor to them and their rules. If you disagree from time to time, then ask, respectfully, to present your point of view. Sometimes parents are busy and say no too quickly, or they might not realize your desires. They will be more likely to reconsider and treat your thoughts with respect if you honor and obey at other times.

Will you try this three-step plan when faced with unpleasant but appropriate requests from your parents?

1. Agree to obey. "Yes, I'll do what you tell me."
2. Ask to present your point of view. "May I first tell you what I'm thinking?"

Chatting With Girls Like You

3. Give your point of view, with respect, and then obey. "Thanks for listening. I'll do whatever you decide."

Children, obey your parents because you belong to the Lord, for this is the right thing to do.
EPHESIANS 6:1A NLT

Family

Can't I stop going to church with my family? It's boring.

One of my favorite books when I was a kid was called *All About Me*. In it I got to write down all of the things I liked best—my favorite colors, my favorite foods, what I wanted my house to look like when I grew up, how many kids I wanted. In the back was a section about my hopes and dreams—including what I wanted my future husband to look like—and also secret fears! I spent a lot of time doodling about myself. But it kept me really focused on *me*.

Some of my friends had *All About Me* books, too. One day we all got brave enough to let one another read our books—after we promised not to tell anyone else what we'd read. One friend was secretly afraid to talk in class. I never knew! Others had similar problems and also funny—and sweet—dreams. Once I stopped thinking all about me and started thinking all about them, my priorities changed. I tried to help my friend feel brave to speak. My friends encouraged me when my baby sister was born and my world changed. One of my friends knew God.

Church, as it turns out, is *not* all about me. First and foremost, it's all about God—learning more about Him, worshiping Him, serving Him, and most important, loving and getting to know Him. After God, it's all about God's people. If you're a Christian, you're one of them. God says things like "Love one another," "Learn the Scripture so you're not ashamed," "Use your gifts to help others." Rather than focusing on what you are *getting* from church, switch your focus to the *All About Him* book—the Bible—and those He's placed you with in Sunday school or in the chair right next to you. That's not just entertainment.

What can you do to make sure you focus on God while you're at church?

Chatting With Girls Like You

Is there someone at church God wants you to befriend and/or serve? Who?

How does changing the focus from "me" to "Him" or "them" change your feelings about church?

> *Let us think about each other and help each other to show love and do good deeds. You should not stay away from the church meetings, as some are doing. But you should meet together and encourage each other.*
> Hebrews 10:24–25

Family

My grandma bought a dress for me. She's asking me if I like it. I don't. What do I say?

Ooh, hard one. Congratulations on both being honest and wanting to do the right thing! When someone gives another person a gift, usually they try to do a few things:

1. Buy or make something that shares a little bit of themselves in the selection.
2. Honor the person for whom the gift is intended by choosing something she would like.
3. Offer it as a celebratory item (like for a birthday or the first day of school) or as a token of love.

You have three choices. One, you could lie to her, tell her you like it so you don't hurt her feelings, but then make her wonder what's up when you never wear it. She's going to figure out somehow that it's not what you had in mind. Then you'll have this awkward little lie between you. Two, you could tell her you don't like it. Flat out, nothing else. Something tells me this would cause some pain and awkwardness, too. Three, you could answer her carefully, thankfully, *and* honestly. Then it will honor both of your real feelings.

You might consider telling your grandma that you are so thankful that she thinks of you and that you know not everyone has a grandma who buys them gifts. Explain that fashions change quickly, and so does your body, so this particular dress won't work. You might suggest spending a few hours shopping together—building your relationship—which will allow you to exchange this dress for something that will work. This allows you to be honest while respecting your grandma's intent in gift giving. It may be awkward at first, but thankful, gentle honesty always builds a relationship after those first few scary moments. Lies, even ones you think are little and said with good intentions, tear relationships down.

Do you ever say you like something when you don't, just so you don't hurt someone else's feelings?

Chatting With Girls Like You

Come up with a sentence here, something you can be prepared to say to show gentle, thankful honesty next time that situation arises.

An honest answer is as pleasing as a kiss on the lips.
PROVERBS 24:26

Family

My sister is a teenager. Even though she doesn't hate me, she says she does. She never wants to be with me. What should I do?

One of the very first poems we learn as little girls is, "Sticks and stones will break my bones, but words will never hurt me." Ouch. It's not true, is it? Sticks and stones cause bruises you see, but they go away in just a few days. Words cause wounds you can't see, but they don't go away for a long time.

When your sister says she hates you, that's gotta hurt. Deep inside her heart, though, she doesn't hate you. You're a wise girl to realize that. As you probably already realize, as you grow older you face bigger challenges. It's not just what kind of lunch box you have anymore; it's who your friends are. It's not if your clothes feel good but if they *look* good. Your sister is probably facing even bigger challenges. Boys. Peer Pressure. Body pressure. Grade pressure. Kermit the Frog sang, "It's not easy being green." It's not easy being a teen, either.

Just knowing that it's the pressure around her that causes her to say and do the things she does—and nothing you yourself are doing—will help ease the hurt. You might talk to her and say, "I really like to spend time with you. When you have some time, or when there's something you want to do with me, let me know." Then let her pick the time and place. Let *her* come back to *you*. Try hard to let those words stop at your skin and not dig into your heart. Be kind, and go out of your way to do something nice for her once in a while to show your love. Then be patient. One day *you* will be the teenager who needs extra understanding, and she'll be a big sister who can guide you through. You've got a lifetime to be sisters. Friends may come and go, but sisters are forever.

What helps you to be patient and kind to people who are being difficult to you?

Chatting With Girls Like You

What can you do to make life easier for your brother or sister, knowing the Lord will reward you for godliness even if your brother or sister doesn't?

It takes wisdom to have a good family. It takes understanding to make it strong.
PROVERBS 24:3

Family

What do you do when you want to have a kind-of boyfriend but your parents won't let you? How can I convince them it's okay?

Babies aren't in this world very long before they figure out there is some pain involved in being a kid! When a baby is only two months old, she starts getting her first shots. Really! I'll bet if you were to ask those babies, "Hey, would you like this long needle poking into your chubby little leg?" the baby would answer, "No way!" But without those shots, babies are vulnerable to a lot of sicknesses—sicknesses that can kill them before they ever get to be adults.

I didn't ask my kids if they wanted a shot. I knew what they needed, and I made sure they got it. Sure, it was hard for me to watch. The look those babies gave me—whew! It was like, "Aren't you supposed to be helping me, not hurting me?" Now that my kids are older, though, they know that when they need a shot it's a little bit of a pinch that will save them a whole lot of pain later on. They trust me to help them decide what they need, even if it's going to hurt for a time.

Parents don't only protect you from physical pain. They also want to protect you from emotional pain. Sometimes that means saying no to a bad friendship. Sometimes it might mean telling you you're not old enough yet to have a boyfriend, even a kind-of boyfriend. A teacher may like you, a neighbor may like you, a friend may like you, but your parents would give their lives for you. They are much more bound to you and are willing to suffer the pain of your unhappiness and anger now if they need to in order to guide you for your long-term good. They try to protect like Jesus, the true Good Shepherd, would.

Chatting With Girls Like You

In an area that you disagree with your parents on (boys, curfew, phone or computer use, etc.), respectfully ask your parents why they've set the guidelines they have. See if you can come to an agreement on how to proceed.

My area of discussion will be . . .

Are there times when you've had to tell someone something that you knew might hurt him or her, but you did it anyway for the person's own good? Who? When?

> *The good shepherd gives his life for his sheep. The worker who is paid to keep the sheep is different from the shepherd who owns them. So when the worker sees a wolf coming, he runs away and leaves the sheep alone. Then the wolf attacks the sheep and scatters them. The man runs away because he is only a paid worker. He does not really care for the sheep.*
> JOHN 10:11B–13

Part Five

Society

You are the salt of the earth. But what good is salt if it has lost its flavor? Can you make it useful again? It will be thrown out and trampled underfoot as worthless. You are the light of the world—like a city on a mountain, glowing in the night for all to see. Don't hide your light under a basket! Instead, put it on a stand and let it shine for all. In the same way, let your good deeds shine out for all to see, so that everyone will praise your heavenly Father.

MATTHEW 5:13–16

Girls Like You Wonder...

1. It confuses me when adults lie. Why do they do that?

2. Why can't people say "I'm sorry" when they should?

3. How can I help my neighbors understand God?

4. I'm totally worried about being kidnapped. What should I do?

5. Should I be afraid? My family is in debt.

6. What can I do when people say "Oh my God"?

7. I'm concerned that my mom and dad might lose their jobs. What would we do?

8. What are "gay" people?

9. What should I do if people I love don't respect our leaders?

10. Why do people demolish trees and fields to make new houses?

Society

Sometimes adults lie. That confuses me, because then I don't know what the truth is.

When I was a kindergartner, I thought that fourth graders knew it all. There was a fourth grader at my bus stop. Her ponytail was always smooth, and she wore "big girl" clothes. When a boy pestered me, she wasn't afraid to step in and help. She had all the answers. She'd always do the right thing. Or so I thought. When I was in sixth grade, though, I knew for sure that fourth graders did *not* know it all. After all, I'd already been a fourth grader who'd made a few mistakes and bad choices.

When you're a kid, it can seem like adults know and will always do the right thing. I remember believing that all old people were kind. Well, guess what? If they were kind young people, they grew into kind old people. If they were crabby young people, they generally made for crabby old people. Being an adult—or old—doesn't guarantee good character. Good character means telling the truth, self-sacrifice, hard, diligent work, considering others before oneself, being kind, etc. Lots of kids do those things. Some kids don't. Lots of adults do those things. Some adults don't.

In the book of Acts, Paul talked to people every day about the right things to do. Some of the people he talked to, the Bereans, would go home and check with the Scriptures to make sure the things he was saying were true. They wanted to make sure, before they acted on anything, that they were hearing the truth. They didn't believe Paul only because he was an authority. They checked with other reliable sources, too.

When an adult tells you something, it's okay to go to a second reliable source and make sure it's true. The Scripture, of course, is the best place for truth. Just ask the Bereans! Your parents, your Sunday school teacher, or the Christian parent of a friend is okay, too. Be open and willing to be taught. But be wise, and if something doesn't sound right, respectfully check it out. Fourth graders tell the truth most of the time. Most adults do, too. Sometimes bad choices or mistakes are made. It's okay to verify.

Chatting With Girls Like You

What are three good resources or people you can use to make sure you believe the truth?

1.

2.

3.

Who said, "I am the way, the truth, and the life"?
(Hint: Read John 14:6 NLT.)

Good people are guided by their honesty; treacherous people are destroyed by their dishonesty.
PROVERBS 11:3 NLT

Society

Why don't people say "I'm sorry" when they should?

Hey, who *does* like to admit they are wrong? No one that I know. We fear that the people we have wronged won't like us anymore. We worry that we will lose their respect. We worry that there will be consequences, and sometimes there are! Sometimes, though, we just don't think that what we did was a "big deal." It's one way of saying that our sin isn't so bad.

In Matthew 18, Jesus tells the story of a man who owed a debt to the king. The king began to collect his money. This man owed the king a lot of money! But he pleaded with the king to forgive him his debt—meaning he wouldn't have to pay. The king kindly forgave the debt. That man then turned to someone who owed *him* money. Did he forgive that man the very small amount owed? No! He treated him harshly, throwing him into prison. The man whom the king had forgiven did not see the truth—that he was willing to be forgiven but not to forgive. When the king found out, boy, he was mad. He put that man into prison, too.

A wise and generous person realizes that he has to both ask for forgiveness and give forgiveness. We all make mistakes. Be humble when you do wrong. Say you are sorry and ask for forgiveness. Both parts are important. Saying you're sorry is great, but it doesn't restore the relationship. Only when forgiveness is asked for and granted is that relationship made right. Next time someone sins against you, forgive her, too. Hopefully she'll be wise enough to say she is sorry and ask for forgiveness. But if she isn't, remember the lesson your Lord taught. Offer forgiveness anyway and model the right thing to do.

When you say you're sorry to someone, do you always ask for forgiveness, too? Why or why not?

Chatting With Girls Like You

Do you need to wait till people say they are sorry before you can forgive them?

What happens inside of you when you truly forgive someone?

> *Be kind and loving to each other. Forgive each other just as God forgave you in Christ.*
> EPHESIANS 4:32

Society

I would like my neighbors to know the Lord. What should I do first?

It's really cool when you realize that God has placed certain people in your neighborhood. It's no accident that they're there and so are you. God says you are the light that lights up the world. Light makes things grow. Light brings happiness. Light shows the way. Girls like you want to be lights in your world. How can you be this light?

Jesus tells us the story of the Good Samaritan. The Samaritan came across a man lying in a road, hurt. The Samaritan might be late for his appointment, lose business, or not make it home on time if he stopped to help. But he did not put his interests first. He didn't even put a friend's interests first. He put a stranger first. The Samaritan helped the hurt man, took care of his needs, and then made sure he was safe and well cared for. He didn't get anything in return. He didn't ask for anything in return. Maybe he didn't even get thanked! He did show unconditional love, which means loving someone without expecting anything at all—not even love or a thank-you—in return.

That's how God loves us, and it's radical and different. When you start loving people without expecting anything in return, people stop and notice. Why? It hardly ever happens. Then they want to know *why* you do that. Your friends and neighbors might come out and ask you, "Why did you bring me cookies?" or ". . . get my toddler's ball?" or ". . . water my plants without pay when we were on vacation?" If you tell them you do it because you're a Christian, you will be showing them the same kind of love that Jesus shows you. Even if they don't come right out and ask you why, they'll see you going to church, wearing a cross, and using His name in conversation. They'll get the picture. You're different. The word *Christian* means to be like Christ. As Christ shows unconditional love for you, you show it to your neighbor. Heads and hearts will turn.

Chatting With Girls Like You

What are five things you can do to show love to your neighbors?

1.

2.

3.

4.

5.

Will you commit to doing one of these things today or tomorrow? If so, sign here:

In the same way, you should be a light for other people. Live so that they will see the good things you do. Live so that they will praise your Father in heaven.
MATTHEW 5:16

Society

I worry that I might get kidnapped or that something else bad might happen to me.

Television, newspapers, and radios are in the business of making money. If a story catches people's attention, it sells advertising space. Therefore, a lot of attention is focused on the bad and not very much on the good. Try this: Focus on an object across the room. Stare at it. You'll notice, out of the corner of your eye, the other things in the room, but everything will be centered on what you're focusing on. It's not that it is bigger—it's just getting all the attention. Whatever you focus on will take over your thoughts.

There are bad people in this world, and some of them do bad things. Mostly, though, there are kind people. I lost my debit card last week and worried that someone would use it before I got it back. No one did. That very same day I found a ten-dollar bill on the sidewalk in front of Safeway and turned it in to customer service. Both the person who found my card and I had the opportunity to do something bad, but we didn't.

Think about it like this: There are 365 days in a year, and maybe five of them have really bad weather. You might have thunderstorms where you live, or hurricanes or blizzards. If people prepare themselves and their homes, though, most are perfectly safe inside while the storm whirls around them. They also don't spend the other days worrying about possible bad weather next month. In the same way, there are bad things and bad people in this world. Scary things happen to everyone from time to time, many of them hurtful. However, worrying won't help. What can you do? Take some safety precautions—don't walk alone, always be in before dark, follow your parents' instructions. Listen when people at home, school, or church teach you about protecting yourself. Be smart. Ask questions when something feels uncomfortable. After you've done all you can do, though, set it aside. Focus on God and His ability to protect you from evil and restore you if something does happen, not on potential problems. Whatever you focus on—either His peace or the problems around you—will be the biggest influence on your mood.

Chatting With Girls Like You

What do you fear? What steps can you take to act wisely to protect yourself from that?

Why does God tell you to give thanks at the same time that you're asking Him to help you with your needs?

> *Do not worry about anything. But pray and ask God for everything you need. And when you pray, always give thanks. And God's peace will keep your hearts and minds in Christ Jesus. The peace that God gives is so great that we cannot understand it.*
> PHILIPPIANS 4:6–7

Society

What does it mean to be in debt?

Being in debt means to owe somebody something. You can owe them money, a favor, or work. Have you ever heard someone say, "I'll do this for you, but you owe me big time!" That means she will do something for you, but she expects you to do something for her the next time she asks.

The problem with debt, whether it's money or love or favors, is that you're not free. If you owe people money, you have to pay them back before you can spend the money on other things. Those things might be something you want or something you'd like to give to others. People who owe a lot of money to credit cards can't give as much to godly causes. They aren't free to. It's always best to stay out of debt. But using a charge card or credit card doesn't necessarily mean going into debt. Debit cards look like credit cards but are actually more like checks—they take money right out of the bank account. Some people charge things to keep track of expenses, but they pay the cards off every month, not making a debt.

One way to stay out of debt with money is to be content with what you have. Learn to be happy with whatever clothing you have, the house you have, the gear your family can afford for you. People who aren't content "charge"—or purchase on credit—what they want before they have the money for it. Charging means getting into debt.

One way to stay out of relationship debt is to make sure that when you do something for or with someone else, there are "no strings attached." That means if you invite someone to your house, it's because you want to spend time with her, not because you expect her to invite you to her great pool the next week. On the other hand, don't ask someone to help you with something if there has to be payback. Ask someone only if she'll help you freely and allow you to do the same. Whomever you're in debt to, you're serving until that debt is paid. Don't become indebted to anyone you don't want to serve.

Chatting With Girls Like You

Do you ever do things for people expecting them to pay you back? What?

Have you asked someone for help, but then she expected you to pay her back? Who? When?

Generally speaking, are you content with your stuff, or do you always want the newest and best? How might that kind of thinking lead to debt later in life?

Just as the rich rule the poor,
so the borrower is servant to the lender.
PROVERBS 22:7 NLT

Society

Why do people think it's okay to say "Oh my God"?

Names are really important. They represent the person or thing that carries the name. One of the ways God showed Adam that He was giving Adam authority and power was by allowing Adam to name the animals. It was an important task.

When you get a new pet, a lot of thought goes into the name. Whenever I write a book, I give a lot of thought to naming the characters. One time I wanted to name the mean girl in a book Lisa. Why? Because when I was a girl, I knew a really mean person named Lisa. To me the name Lisa meant *mean*. When I want to name a kind character, I often choose a name that reminds me of kindness.

God is the "most" of everything good—most powerful, most kind, most wise. His name represents Him, too. The Bible tells us that Jesus is the name above all names. Why? Because Jesus is the One above all others. There is power in the name of God. Like anything else with power, we don't want to misuse it. God deserves all of our respect. Like anyone else's name, God's name represents Him. We don't want to misuse it, either.

How can you misuse God's name? Anytime you use the name of God or Jesus without talking respectfully to or about Him, you're misusing His name. Saying "Oh my God" is not calling upon God. It's misusing His name to show amazement. Some words, such as *golly, gee, gosh,* and *geez* are all slang words for either God or Jesus. People who use them—and even most people who say "Oh my God"—don't really understand what they're doing. They're just using them out of habit. We shouldn't judge those people or think unkindly toward them, but we can set a good example. And if you're close to a person who does use those words, you might gently explain to her why you've chosen not to. You can certainly say "amazing," "incredible," or "wow" with just as much effect. You won't be thoughtlessly misusing the name of the One you love.

Chatting With Girls Like You

Do you ever use the words *golly, gosh, gee,* or *geez?* What other words can you use instead?

How else can someone misuse the name of the Lord?

You must not use the name of the Lord your God thoughtlessly. The Lord will punish anyone who is guilty and misuses his name.
EXODUS 20:7

Society

Could my dad or mom lose his or her job?

Yes, your parents could lose their jobs. In this world, in our society, almost everyone will lose a job at one time or another. If someone loses a job and wasn't expecting to, it's very painful. It feels like rejection. It can make a person very sad, and that's hard to watch. Especially if it's your mom or dad.

Losing a job can also seem scary because you wonder what you will do next. Will your parent get another job? Will it be one that he or she likes? Will there be enough money to live on?

One great truth to hold on to is that God is like a safety net. Have you been to a circus? The trapeze artists get out there and swing, twirl, and jump. They often catch one another as they go from swing to swing. From time to time, though, the acrobats fall. Instead of reaching the swing, they miss their grip. As they fall, it probably feels like they're going to go *splat!* But they know that, ahead of time, someone has strung up safety nets. They will fall, but they won't go *splat*. It will feel scary, but they'll be safe. They can shake themselves off, recover a bit, and try again.

Our lives are like that, too. We go to work and are swinging and twirling and jumping. Occasionally we miss our grip or something out of our control goes wrong. When that happens, a buddy might catch us. But if not, God is our safety net. He will allow us to fall but not go *splat*. He catches us, cares for us, and will take care of our needs. Even if it seems like a looooong time, He helps find a new place for your mom or dad to shine.

Has your mom or dad ever lost a job? How did God take care of your needs during that time?

Chatting With Girls Like You

How is God like a safety net in *your* life?

My God will use his wonderful riches in Christ Jesus to give you everything you need.
PHILIPPIANS 4:19

Society

What are gay people?

Gay is a word that means happy or joyful or carefree. If you read old books or watch older movies, you'll hear the word *gay* being used to describe someone who has those feelings.

Now, though, the word usually means something else. Gay is one way people refer to homosexual people. Homosexual men are attracted to other men, and homosexual women are attracted to other women, in the way that a husband and wife or boyfriend and girlfriend are attracted to each other. It doesn't mean liking other people as friends or roommates, which, of course, is perfectly fine.

Some people say that homosexual people are made that way. It may be true that some people feel more temptation for that than others, but God does not make someone a certain way and then forbid him or her to act on it. The Bible tells us that God forbids homosexuality (Romans 1:26–27), but He allows people to make their own choices about their behavior. The good news is, people can change wrong behavior if they are convicted to do so and they choose to change.

Do you know anyone who is homosexual? If you do, do you pray for that person? Why not do that right now?

> *People did not think it was important to have a true knowledge of God. So God left them and allowed them to have their own worthless thinking. And so those people do the things that they should not do.*
> ROMANS 1:28

Chatting With Girls Like You

It bugs me when people don't respect their leaders. Why does that happen?

Everyone, and everything, needs a leader. God set up the universal laws. He is the ultimate Leader. He delegates work to others. There are always rankings—higher and lower. Did you know there will even be leaders in heaven?

In the animal world there are leaders. The alpha dog is in charge of the pack. The other dogs respect him. If they don't, they're kicked out of the pack. Bees have a queen bee. If they don't respect her, the other bees attack them. Geese fly in the form of a letter V. The leader stays at the front and takes the brunt of the wind for a time and the other geese follow. When that leader is tired, it moves to the back and another goose takes a turn.

Humans need leaders, too. We have laws, most of which are based on laws God set up, and we need to follow them. Leaders help us do that. We need to make new, good laws from time to time to address our world. Leaders help us do that. Sometimes wars or disasters happen. Leaders help us respond to that. God set up His universe to be one of order. Leadership helps keep the order.

Sometimes people don't like the leaders over them. They don't agree with their decisions or their plans or the way they live their lives. As Christians, we might disagree with certain things that our leaders do. But we are to respect the position that the leader has, even when we don't respect the person. When Christians badmouth other people, it just makes them look bad. That's different from honest difference of opinion. Honest difference of opinion is offered with respect. It's okay to disagree with a leader, but it needs to be done with respect. It's okay to wish the rules were different, but until they are, we need to obey them or work to change them. Keep in mind that, like geese, human leaders take on the brunt of the wind in the world around them. They need our prayers till it's their turn to fall to the back of the flock and let someone else take over.

Society

Do you ever talk disrespectfully about those in leadership around you?

If you have an honest differing of opinion, what can you do?

First, I tell you to pray for all people. Ask God for the things people need, and be thankful to him. You should pray for kings and for all who have authority. Pray for the leaders so that we can have quiet and peaceful lives—lives full of worship and respect for God. This is good, and it pleases God our Savior.
1 Timothy 2:1–3

Chatting With Girls Like You

There is a beautiful field in the back of my house that has deer, rabbits, and frogs. They are going to tear it down and build inexpensive houses. Is that right?

God made us to appreciate nature. When I walk through a forest, the many shades of green fall down around me, and the air is cool and sweet. I hear many voices I don't normally hear—chirping, croaking, cricketing. Walking through a field, grass scratching my legs, bugs diving to the sides of my path, I see some of His creatures I don't often see. Taking care of our pet hamster, cupping her in my hand and watching her wash her little face with her paws, brings me great pleasure. God made many creatures and plants, and then He made us. He wants us to take care of them all.

Part of taking care of His creation means we are careful managers. We don't mow down all of the trees. Instead, we cut the ones we need to use, we replant, and we save some for the forest. We carefully plan where houses will be built so as not to use up *all* available land.

But when God made everything, He made an order. In His order, people are more important than plants and animals. People are made in His image. He told people to rule over plants and animals. Although they are important, their needs come after the needs of people.

Maybe there's a girl like you whose family can't afford a home right now, and she will be able to have her own room in the houses they are building behind you. She might even turn out to be a good friend! Perhaps the people who planned your city set aside land for a park or walking trail nearby so that the needs for people's homes and nature can both be met. You can always write a letter to your mayor and ask. Mayors love to get mail from interested kids.

Thank you for being concerned about plants and animals as well as people. You're already doing a great job being a good citizen.

Society

What do you feel like when you're away from the city, in a natural surrounding with plants and trees and lots of insects and animals?

How can you be a good manager of both plants and animals, and the people around you—right now, not just when you grow up?

> "Rule over the fish in the sea and over the birds in the sky. Rule over every living thing that moves on the earth." God said, "Look, I have given you all the plants that have grain for seeds. And I have given you all the trees whose fruits have seeds in them. They will be food for you. I have given all the green plants to all the animals to eat. They will be food for every wild animal, every bird of the air and every small crawling animal."
> And it happened.
> GENESIS 1:28B–30

Part Six

School

A wise person learns from instruction.
Proverbs 21:11b NLT

Girls Like You Wonder...

1. Is it wrong to compare my grades with other people's grades?

2. Why is my teacher so strict?

3. I'm afraid to make mistakes. What can I do?

4. Does God really care about my schoolwork?

5. Why can't some people get their work done on time?

6. Why does the whole class sometimes gets punished for what one person does?

7. Why do people in my school think it's okay to dress inappropriately?

8. Is it okay to slack off just a little if it's to do something good like reading or sports?

9. What can a kid say when a teacher makes fun of her faith?

10. Should I tell a boy at school that I like him?

School

Math is really hard for me. Why do I always compare myself with those who don't have trouble?

Have you heard the saying "The grass is always greener on the other side of the fence"? It means that, when you look across the neighborhood, it always seems as though the other people have better lawns. They water as much as you do, not more. They don't fertilize more. Why is theirs greener?

But looks can be deceptive. I recently read an article that says the reason grass looks greener at a distance is because you can't see the dirt as well. Up close, in your own yard, you can see the dirt intermingled with the grass, bare patches, and moss. From a distance you see only green grass tops. If you went to your neighbor's yard and looked from *her* perspective, your grass might look greener than *hers*. And she wouldn't see your weeds.

It's the same in your life. There are things that come easily for you and things that are more difficult. The difficult things get much more attention than the things that come easily. Whatever we focus on seems to be bigger in our lives—which is why our problems often seem bigger than our blessings. You see the dirt close up! When you look at your friend, you may see her green grass: good math grades, nice hair, cute clothes. But you don't see her weeds: reading trouble, nervousness in speaking, insecure friendships. You can bet *she* sees them, though.

Christians are made to cooperate, not compete. Instead of comparing yourself with others, ask for help. Your friend might be glad to help you with math if you'd help her with language arts. Show her how to pull her hair back into a new ponytail style, and she'll show you a new game. She'll be glad to know that you have problems, and she will feel better about sharing her own. In the process you'll appreciate yourselves and others more because you won't worry about how bad you are and how good they are. You'll be focused on working together.

Chatting With Girls Like You

What school subjects or times in the school day are difficult for you?

Do you have a friend for whom these subjects and times come more easily? Will you ask for help? What help can you offer to her? *(Hint: If you don't know, ask her!)*

Share each other's troubles and problems, and in this way obey the law of Christ. . . . Be sure to do what you should, for then you will enjoy the personal satisfaction of having done your work well, and you won't need to compare yourself to anyone else.
GALATIANS 6:2, 4 NLT

School

I have a really strict teacher. She doesn't ever bend the rules, even though I think she should sometimes.

Toddlers can't understand the fence around the playground. Look at those great trees to climb—just outside the fence. And a pond—with ducks to feed! But toddlers don't see the street between the fence and the trees. They don't know how to swim and don't understand that falling into the pond could kill them. The fence is there for their protection. They just don't understand it yet.

That's how it is with rules. Rules are like fences: *Don't go here. Don't turn this way. Danger over here.* Rules protect you. Rules that protect you physically are pretty easy to understand. You know, of course, why people can't wander across a road. Rules that protect your spirit and your mind are harder to understand, because you can't see your spirit or your mind like you can see your body.

When we cross one of God's laws, the Bible calls it sin. It's such a bad thing that the Lord says sin leads us to death. Sin leads to death of our spirit. If we are Christians, sin will lead us away from God. If we turn back and follow His rules and His plan, it leads to life. Following rules in one area of your life makes it easy to follow them in other areas of your life. Bending rules in one area of your life makes it easier to bend them in another area of your life.

If you skip over work or cheat, or your teacher gives you a grade you don't deserve, it doesn't help your mind. Your brain will not understand the work it needs to understand in order to learn the next topic. It may seem easy at the moment, but it will make the next work harder and harder, till you can't go any further. Maybe your teacher's rules protect your mind from things you shouldn't see. The rules may protect you from lazy habits that will lead to poor grades.

If your teacher sets rules, they are for your good. Maybe they'll protect you physically. Maybe they'll protect you spiritually. Maybe they'll protect your mind. Stay inside the fences set for you and have a good time growing and learning. The fences will get farther and farther apart as you grow older. By then you'll be ready to run.

Chatting With Girls Like You

Does your teacher have rules that are hard for you to follow or seem dumb or silly? Name one or two:

1.

2.

Now think of one possible but legitimate thing that each of these rules could be protecting you from—either physically or emotionally, stopping a bad habit from developing, whatever!

1.

2.

My child, hold on to wisdom and reason. Don't let them out of your sight! . . . Then you will go on your way in safety. And you will not get hurt.
PROVERBS 3:21, 23

School

How can I feel unafraid to make mistakes, especially with new things I am learning, when I don't feel I'm very good?

The reason so many of us are afraid of making mistakes is because it means we'll look dumb to others—*What will they think?* Or because we are worried that it means we really *are* dumb—*I'm not performing too well.* A book called *The Search for Significance,* by Robert McGee, puts it this way: The world says my worth is my performance plus what other people think about me. *Real* self-worth is what God gives you. He made you. He loves you. He doesn't expect you to be perfect. He chose you, and He already knows that you will never be perfect here on earth.

Have you ever thought about diamonds? Really, they're just rocks, minerals in the ground. Sure, they're really pretty when they're polished. But so are rose quartz, agates, and jade. Why are diamonds more valuable, more sought after? Because people decided they liked them and the diamonds were valuable to them. Diamonds don't really do anything. People who choose diamonds value them simply because they want to.

You are very much like a diamond. There is nothing that you have to do to be valuable. You are valuable because God made you. He loves you. He chose you. When you are certain about that, you will realize that you don't have to be the best in order to have worth. It doesn't matter what other people think about you. You are free to try anything righteous and then to either succeed or to fail. Neither success nor failure makes you more precious to God. You are precious because you're the treasure of His heart.

What would you like to try but are afraid to because of fear of failure?

Chatting With Girls Like You

What's the worst that can happen? Can you live with that?

What's the best that could happen? Are you willing to take a risk, knowing your real worth, in order to try?

> *And this hope will never disappoint us, because God has poured out his love to fill our hearts. God gave us his love through the Holy Spirit, whom God has given to us. Christ died for us while we were still weak. We were living against God, but at the right time, Christ died for us. . . . Christ died for us while we were still sinners. In this way God shows his great love for us.*
> ROMANS 5:5–6, 8

School

Does God really care about my schoolwork?

Yes! God cares about every little thing about you. The Bible tells us that God knit you together in your mother's womb. Have you ever seen someone knit?

First, the knitter envisions her product. She decides what she wants to make—a sweater, a scarf, a blanket. She determines what color would be best. It might depend on where she's going to place it—brown would look lovely for a blanket in the living room, peach perhaps for a sweater. Will it need to be lightweight yarn so it can be used all year? Heavier, for winter only? Next, she purchases all of her supplies. She keeps them in a safe, clean place to protect them. She wants the final product to reflect her forethought, her concern, her care, and her craft. When she finishes her knitting, it will be beautiful. The creation reflects the maker.

Sometimes the sweater or blanket has a pull in it. The yarn becomes tangled or the pattern crooked. When that happens, the knitter goes back, undoes the mistake, and redoes it till it's right. In the same way, *you* are God's creation. He thought about you before you were created. He planned you with a special beauty in mind. He wants everything you do and everything you are to reflect Him and His intentions for you. Does He expect you to be perfect in every way? No! But when He sees something that isn't just right in your life, He will stop until you and He correct the imperfection. Then you'll move on.

Just like that, your work reflects who *you* are. When you work carefully, with forethought, concern, and care, it tells about you as a person. You do good work. You care about what kind of reports you turn in. You study for a test because it shows that you are diligent and prepared. When you make a mistake, you go back and fix it. Not everyone can get an A for achievement, but we can all get an A for effort. A blanket reflects the care of its creator. Your attitude and effort shows what kind of a person you are. Your diligent work reflects honor to your Maker.

Chatting With Girls Like You

What subjects do you try really hard at? What subjects are you tempted to slack off in?

Can everyone control their grades for achievement most of the time? Can you control the quality of your attitude and effort most of the time?

In all the work you are doing, work the best you can.
Work as if you were working for the Lord, not for men.
Remember that you will receive your reward from the
Lord, which he promised to his people.
You are serving the Lord Christ.
COLOSSIANS 3:23–24

School

I never get my work done on time. What can I do?

Last year my family watched The Gentleman Jugglers. They are two guys who have been friends for a really long time—since they were kids! They started their act by tossing one ball into the air, then two, then three, till they had worked up to six or seven balls. When it became too much for one of them, he would toss one or two of the balls to his friend, the other Gentleman Juggler. That man would juggle the balls till his friend was able to handle them again. Once the first guy had his routine under control, his partner would toss the fifth and sixth balls back to him. Maybe more!

All of the many things in your life are like those balls. Time with God is one; so are time with your family and homework. You could keep adding lots of really good activities and things to do. But even if they are all good things, at some point you're going to have too many balls. Then they'll come crashing down, and they'll all be on the ground. When we are doing too many things, we often have time to start many of them but complete none of them—not in a timely manner or as a job well done. Late homework, missed practices, not enough practice time for instruments, staying up too late to get things done, messy rooms—all of those things are signs of too many activities.

If you're not getting your schoolwork done on time, maybe you're doing too many things. School is your "job" right now. After God and your family, it needs to have priority. Why not ask your mom or dad to help you decide which three or four balls you can handle well right now? Then, when you have them all going in a rhythm, you can ask your mom or dad to toss another ball your way.

If you're forced to temporarily give something up that you really like, say a sport or music, it will motivate you to get your work done on time. Showing yourself to be responsible to complete your work on time will convince your mom and dad that they can toss another ball your way—something you'd *really* like to do.

Chatting With Girls Like You

How many activities do you have this week? List sports, practices, church and church activities, time with family, time with friends, music, school-related events—everything.

If you dropped one of these activities, would you have more time for your homework? Which subject needs more attention? Would you have more time for important relationships? Which ones need more attention (God, parents, siblings . . .)?

It is better to finish something than to start it.
ECCLESIASTES 7:8A

School

What can you do when the whole class gets punished for something that just one or two people did?

It's a bummer when you get punished for something someone else did. It doesn't seem fair. Part of the problem, though, is that we are always looking for what is fair. Hey, how can *that* be a problem?

Well, what is fair, anyway? My family got free tickets to a circus because one member did some community service. We all got to go—even though we didn't all serve. No one worried about fairness then! Likewise, if one person is driving poorly and causes a crash, the entire family can be hurt, though they did nothing wrong. When we spend time looking for things to be fair, it distracts us from our real mission as Christians, which is to be more like Jesus. In the book of Matthew, Jesus tells us to not always worry about life being fair. In fact, He says if someone takes your shirt, give him your coat, too. He's not telling us to let others take advantage of us all the time. He's saying to be different. Be generous. Be kind when it's not called for. When we do these things, we will be different from others. People will wonder why. Then we can tell them why.

God is kind to those who don't deserve it. He says he sends sun and rain—both necessary for life—to both good people and bad people. He sends good things to those who don't deserve it. The fact that Jesus died for you while you were a sinner tells us that God is more interested in what's best than what's fair.

If you're unfairly punished, it's okay to talk with the teacher about it—quietly and respectfully. But remember, the way you handle the situation will tell others a lot about you, your character, your faith, your God. If you do it well, your God will bless you (1 Peter 3).

What good can come of a situation where you feel that you're treated unfairly?

Chatting With Girls Like You

Can you come up with a good way to start a conversation in which you'd like to respectfully disagree with an adult?

Your Father causes the sun to rise on good people and on bad people. Your Father sends rain to those who do good and to those who do wrong.
MATTHEW 5:45B

School

Other people around me at school don't dress appropriately. What can I do?

It can be hard to be modest in an immodest world. New fashions leave more and more skin showing. Sometimes it seems as if a girl has to choose between being grungy or being immodest.

One of the things immodest clothing does is force others to look at what you're trying to say with your style. Are you trying to say "I'm sporty" or "I'm fashionable" or "I'm sexy"? That's what immodest clothing does. It encourages people to look at a girl's body.

Sometimes girls dress inappropriately because they don't know any better. Maybe their moms or sisters dress that way, too. We can't expect people to behave as Christians if they aren't Christians. Girls can be catty and mean about other girls. Don't do it. Don't gossip about those girls, give them rude looks, or even dis them in your mind or your heart. That's being judgmental. You don't want to be held accountable for things you don't yet know, do you? Even Christian girls might not have reached the same understanding of modesty yet that you have.

What *can* you do? You can model a healthy, fashionable, modest style with joy. The Bible says that Christians can influence others by modeling good behavior; persuade people by the way you live. You can act kindly, so that your inner beauty is in line with your outer beauty. Develop your own fun sense of style. Mix and match cute but appropriate clothing. Find a hairstyle using clips or flips that is uniquely you.

Whenever you're tempted to judge someone or talk about her because of her clothing choices, pray for her instead. Just a quick prayer, in your mind. You'll be surprised by how gossiping about someone hardens your heart toward her, but praying for her softens your heart toward her.

Are you tempted to gossip about or look down on inappropriately dressed girls?

Chatting With Girls Like You

Write out a prayer for one of them (you don't need to use her name if someone shares your book).

What is one clothing style or hairstyle that looks really good on you?

I also want women to wear clothes that are right for them. They should dress with respect and right thinking.
1 TIMOTHY 2:9A

School

I love to read a lot, so I would rather read than do my other work—and I get into trouble. But reading is good, right?

Yes, reading is good. Reading is educational, but reading is also entertaining. Just like anything else you do for fun, reading has to have its proper place.

We all need to sleep. In fact, people will begin to show signs of mental illness if they don't get enough sleep! They can't concentrate, speak well, or think straight. However, if people get too much sleep, that's not good for them, either. They grow lazy, the Bible says, and eventually won't be able to eat. You know that you need to eat each and every day. Your body uses food for fuel to think and work and keep running. If you eat too much, though, it will be bad for your body, not good. That's called gluttony, and it will slow your body down and cause it to work too hard.

When you neglect your schoolwork or chores for reading, it's really not choosing to spend time doing something good. First, it's disobedience, because you're not doing the things you've been asked to do. Next, it's spending time doing something fun rather than work, which will lead to laziness. Ouch! There should be a certain amount of time set aside each day and each week for you to do what you please. If you don't feel that you have time for that, speak with your mom and dad about helping you set a time balance. Then, if you choose to read or play or draw or watch TV during that time, it'll be truly *free* time because you'll have met all of your obligations first.

Do you make sure your work is completed on time? What stands in your way, if anything?

Chatting With Girls Like You

Do you have enough free time? If not, will you talk with your mom and dad about it, to help you keep a balanced life?

Try to avoid going too far in doing anything. Those who honor God will avoid doing too much of anything.
ECCLESIASTES 7:18

School

What do I do when a teacher makes jokes about Christians and the Creation?

Interestingly, the way that you defend your beliefs starts way before a teacher makes a joke or tears your faith down. And it starts with you, not your teacher. How? You've been building a relationship with your teacher all year. Your attitude in class, the quality of your work, your tone of voice, and your word choices all talk to your teacher with words or without. You might be saying, "I'm responsible. I'm kind. I do thorough work." Or, if you haven't been doing so well in class, you might be telling the teacher, "I don't like this subject so I'm not trying. I would rather talk with a friend or pass notes than listen to you. This subject bores me, and I'm not afraid to show it." Whatever you've been "telling" your teacher, using words or not, is going to play a big role when an important moment comes.

And it will come. Trust me.

While some teachers are Christians, or are sensitive to matters of faith, some are not. At some point a teacher may use the Lord's name in vain, or the "correct" answer to a test question might go against your Christian beliefs. At that moment all the things you've been telling the teacher are going to go before you. Then you must go and talk with the teacher privately.

The Bible tells us that when we have a problem, we should bring it up privately and respectfully. Approach your teacher, ask him or her if you can talk privately, and then share your concerns like this: "I'm really learning a lot in your class. Thank you. I wanted to tell you that I'm a Christian, and when you make fun of Christians, it troubles me. I know you wouldn't want to hurt my feelings, so I wanted to let you know. Thanks." Sound hard? It really, really is. Even most adults avoid conflict. But when you lovingly speak the truth to someone, you show them respect. You're stronger. You will walk away from that feeling strong. You will have made an impact for Christ in your world. You rock!

Chatting With Girls Like You

Do you know anyone who tears down your faith, makes fun of your beliefs, or uses the Lord's name in vain?

How can you prepare yourself to speak truthfully and lovingly the next time that happens? *(I always ask someone to help me think it through; it's easier with two. . . .)*

Always be ready to answer everyone who asks you to explain about the hope you have. But answer in a gentle way and with respect. Always feel that you are doing right. Then, those who speak evil of your good life in Christ will be made ashamed.
1 PETER 3:15B–16

School

There is this boy I like, and I'm too shy to tell him. I'm afraid he will laugh at me or tell everyone at school. What do I do?

You're getting to the age now where boys are a little more interesting. Just as you might look at a room full of girls and choose only a few who interest you as good friends, you will feel the same about boys. Some will irritate you, some you'll barely notice, some will be good friends, some might seem even more special. That's okay.

As you grow, though, you'll meet many boys. You'll probably like quite a few of them. Some you may like for only a day or two—before he does something obnoxious and you don't like him anymore! Some you may like for a month or a year. As you move into different classes or schools, or even discover more about yourself, you will probably change your mind about him, too.

Because you're just finding out what you do and don't like, it's best not to talk about it too widely. It's always good to talk with your mom, and it's okay to talk with a close friend or two, too—if they can be trusted to not pass on the information! If you go ahead and tell the boy, though, or others, you might be sorry. He might laugh, as you said, or tell others. Then not only will you be embarrassed now, but when you like someone else instead, and you will, it will be even more awkward.

At your age it's normal to be interested in boys but not to date or make any big statements about it. Think inside about what you enjoy about this boy—his sense of humor, his kindness, his friendly smile—but it's probably best to keep the thoughts among you, your parents, and a close friend. That way, when you like someone else, you're free to privately consider a change of mind, too.

Chatting With Girls Like You

Who are the two or three people you feel most comfortable sharing your deepest thoughts and feelings with?

1.

2.

3.

Do you think God is interested in hearing about why you like a certain boy? If God says that He wants to be your friend (and He does say that), would He be open to talking about that with you?

> *If you talk a lot, you are sure to sin.*
> *If you are wise, you will keep quiet.*
> PROVERBS 10:19

Drum roll, please,
for Question 61!

I have a question about something, but I didn't see it in Chatting With Girls Like You. *What should I do?*

You can always ask your parents, a Sunday school teacher, a youth pastor, an aunt, the Christian mother of a friend, or another godly person you know. Look up the topic in a Bible concordance—there is probably one in the back of your Bible. Or check out the first book in this series, *Girl Talk,* to see if it's addressed in there. If you have a question that you think other girls would like to see asked and answered, too, you can write to me at the address below. I won't be able to answer individual questions, but who knows? It might show up in a new book and help thousands of girls—just like you!

> Sandra Byrd
> P.O. Box 822
> Ravensdale, WA 98051

Just for *Girls!*

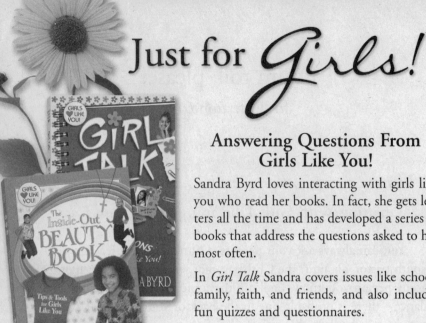

Answering Questions From Girls Like You!

Sandra Byrd loves interacting with girls like you who read her books. In fact, she gets letters all the time and has developed a series of books that address the questions asked to her most often.

In *Girl Talk* Sandra covers issues like school, family, faith, and friends, and also includes fun quizzes and questionnaires.

In *The Inside-Out Beauty Book* Sandra looks at health, beauty, and how to not lose focus on staying beautiful inside.

Join the fun and see what girls like you across the country are talking about!

A Winning Series About Fun and Friends!

Sandra Byrd's HIDDEN DIARY series follows two new friends who have found an antique diary whose pages will lead them on countless adventures and mysteries. Join along and treasure both the friendship as well as the timeless, godly messages in each book.

—THE HIDDEN DIARY by Sandra Byrd

BETHANY HOUSE
www.bethanyhouse.com